# Whisk it All

J.S. WOOD

Copyright © 2018 J.S. Wood
WHISK IT ALL

All rights reserved. No part of this publication may be reproduced, distributed, or transmitted in any form or by any means, including photocopying, recording, or other electronic or mechanical methods, without the prior written permission of the publisher, except in the case of brief quotations embodied in critical reviews and certain other noncommercial uses permitted by copyright law.

This is a work of fiction. Names, characters, places, brands, media, and incidents are either the product of the author's imagination or are used fictitiously. The author acknowledges the trademarked status and trademark owners of various products referenced in this work of fiction, which have been used without permission. The publication and use of these trademarks is not authorized, associated with, or sponsored by the trademark owners.
Published: J.S. Wood Books LLC 2018
authorjswood@gmail.com
Editing: Editing by C. Marie
Cover Design: Star Child Designs
WARNING: This book contains subject matter that may be sensitive for some readers. For mature audiences only (18 and older).

# Whisk It All

## J.S. WOOD

# CHAPTER ONE

*Aveline*

THE MOST EXCITING thing to ever happen in Acton, Colorado, was when the mayor came out. I think his speech was something like, "I'm gay. Get over it."

Okay, so it wasn't exactly like that, but you get my point.

Acton isn't exactly the most happening place in the world...or even in the state. Sometimes they pretend we're interesting by announcing who had the best cookies at the elementary school bake sale or publishing a newspaper about three people read.

It was silly, really, but what are you gonna do? Tell the ninety-year-old man who writes it to retire? No, no we are not gonna do that.

I have lived in Acton my entire life: twenty-one years, six months, and a handful of days. My mother, brother, and I live with my grandparents in a moderately sized farmhouse near the mountains. There is only one house within a few miles of it, and the owner, Old Carl Bernard, passed away a few months ago. It has sat empty ever since. Even when he was alive, Old Carl hardly spoke to anyone, mostly keeping to himself, so we really feel pretty isolated out there.

My grandparents have lived in the home forever, my mom grew up in there, and eventually, my brother, Luke, and I did as well.

It's a beautiful white house with a deck that wraps around the entire perimeter, complete with a front porch swing and rocking chairs, and it has a blue front door with shutters to match. It has its flaws, of course, but it is a dream home for my grandma.

Today I am busy at work on my usual Monday shift, getting the store ready for the day. My mother owns a bakery in town, and I work there on the regular, trying desperately to save money so I can finally leave and see something outside of Colorado.

It's a cloudy day in April, and the promise of a spring snowstorm to come hangs in the air, the dark clouds a sign of impending snow.

I hear the bell ding, indicating customers have entered, and I work my way from the back where I was washing pans from a morning of baking. When I get to the front, I see Sally and Meryl perusing the selection of goodies I made today. The gift of baking was passed down generously from my mother, and I use it wisely.

"Morning ladies," I say as I refill my coffee cup. They are regulars and happen to be the town gossips, so it is always a fun conversation whenever they come in.

Meryl writes for the Acton Gazette along with the aforementioned ninety-year-old man, and she does the gossip column—excuse me, the "local news".

Last I knew, Johnny Mele dancing with Amber Blacker while dating Katie Renner was not news.

"Oh, Aveline!" Sally says when she looks up. I like her. She works at the florist's shop part time and isn't even close to the gossip Meryl is, though she doesn't mind listening in.

"How are you today?" I ask in a casual tone. They do always give me the scoop, which I enjoy. If a woman ever says she doesn't like gossip, she's lying. Just because she doesn't do anything with it doesn't mean she doesn't want to know the good stuff.

"Good, good. Oh my, Belle has outdone herself," Meryl declares as she surveys the spread. My mother, MaeBelle Montgomery, is the sole creator behind Belle's Bakery. She opened it shortly after my father, Jackson, passed. His death was a total shock to us, as he was the healthiest person in our family. He jogged every morning, ate a balanced diet, and only ever indulged in my mother's delicious baked goods.

So, six years ago when he had a brain aneurism, we were devastated. He was the ideal father and husband, supporting each of our ambitions and hobbies and never forcing my brother or me to do anything we didn't want to, though he was always very strict with homework. As a husband, I don't think my mother could've had anyone better, and I think she would agree with me. He was spontaneous and fun, took her on a date night every week, sent her flowers, and overall, he participated in all our lives.

He had a small life insurance policy my mother used to open this place, and one year after opening, it was struggling. My mother had put every dime she'd earned back into bills to the point that it was either lose the bakery or sell our house.

It was an easy decision after my grandmother said we could live at the farm.

Recently, business has picked up and taken off. Mom goes to every local event trying to get the word out, and it works. We get visitors from far and wide looking for the best sweet treats in northern Colorado.

"Today we've whipped up her new peanut butter caramel muffins." I tune back in to the conversation, pointing out the newest creation.

"Oh my, my teeth shake just thinking about those!" Meryl makes this face like she's in deep thought—one she makes often—and I'm endlessly curious as to what could possibly be so difficult. It's just a pastry choice, not her next house. Okay, maybe she gets on my nerves…just a *little*. "I'll take two!" she says, holding up her fingers while I try to hold back an eye roll.

After serving them the coffee and muffins at one of the small tables scattered throughout the shop, they catch me in conversation before I'm able to scurry away.

"So, tell us!" The ladies look at me as if I'm about to tell them I was nominated for an Oscar.

"Tell you…what?" I ask, confused. Meryl gives me a

knowing look while Sally digs into her muffin without a care in the world. I always knew I liked her best.

"About your new neighbor! You know, the one living at Old Carl's place." Hearing her call him Old Carl out loud makes me feel bad about saying it all these years—not bad enough to stop, but...

"Well, I had no idea. I must have been too busy to notice." I did notice. I saw the car in the driveway on my way to work this morning; I just had no idea who it was.

"Well, rumor has it..." *Here we go*, I think as Meryl launches into her 'news'. Apparently, my new neighbor—though it's hard to call him a neighbor when he lives ten miles away—is Old Carl's only nephew. It took him this long to get here because he was in the military, but his uncle left him the house and he is temporarily living there. Turns out he was medically discharged after sustaining some serious injuries.

After the longer-than-necessary conversation with Sally and Meryl, I get back to the kitchen to prep for lunch. I nod at Sunny, our chef in the kitchen who is currently in culinary school. She's awesome, and though she's only been with us a few months, I hope she never leaves.

I really enjoy working for my mother's bakery and eventually I'll be taking it over, but first I want to see the world. I've been saving for it since I was sixteen, envisioning a trip through Europe to start. I spent most of my days in high school with a book glued to my hand, learning everything I needed to know about the places to see and visit and what to avoid. I am prepared to leave this year sometime, I just haven't figured out the *when* yet.

When Mom opened her bakery, I jumped at the chance to work and start saving. At first it wasn't much, but I slowly started building my savings account. My whole family knows of my plans, and my mom in particular has always rooted for me to spread my wings and see the world.

"Never settle." That's what she's always told me. I don't think she ever regretted marrying my dad, her high school sweetheart, but she does tell me to take care of myself first and foremost.

With everything ready in the kitchen, I decide to check out what's on the menu for tomorrow. My mom writes out all her new recipes every month, and we make a new one every week to bring in new customers and keep repeat customers coming back. As I am reading the ingredients for tomorrow, Kate comes running into the kitchen with a huge grin taking over her face.

Kate is our new girl, but a close friend of my brother's, and so far, she manages the register perfectly. She graduated high school last year and since her ambitions change frequently, she decided to hold off on college for now. She was the class clown and is always trying to make people laugh, even if some of her jokes are wildly inappropriate.

"What's up? Your pants on fire?" I ask with a smile.

She shakes her head at me like it was a legitimate question. "More like my panties!" she says in a hushed tone. I purse my lips and hold back a retort. This girl and her inappropriate comments. "Oh man, Ave, you have to see this!" Her excitement piques my curiosity so naturally I follow her to the front of the shop, and she goes straight to the register when we see more customers come in. I scour the bakery, wondering what she saw, and when I look over at her with the silent question on my face, she discreetly points to the back corner. Then I see him.

Now, I'm no prude. I may have only been with one person, but it's not like I haven't seen *Magic Mike*. I know how and when to appreciate a good-looking man, and the man currently sitting in this bakery is by far the most gorgeous man I've ever seen in person. (Credit where credit is due, Mr. Tatum.)

He sits with a book in his hand but is leaning on his elbows, looking out the window. He seems like he's deep in thought with his brows furrowed and his eyes worried. I am surprised it took me so long to notice him.

Kate wasn't lying—he is something to look at, no doubt.

"Here." Kate hands me a cup of coffee. I look at her, confused, and she rolls her eyes. *Too much time in my company.* "It's his! Go deliver it and say hi." Her eyes look eager, like she is about to get a piece of candy.

"Why don't you do it? There's no reason for me to."

She rolls her eyes again. "Ave, he's new, and you're the daughter of the owner. Go welcome him." With that she pushes me in his direction. I slowly walk over, careful not to trip over my feet. He must sense me coming because he looks up and locks his bright blue eyes with mine. I try not to stop and gasp at how pretty they are.

I finally reach his table and can't help but stare at him and admire his features. He clears his throat and I snap out of it then set his coffee down.

"Hello." Even his voice is beautiful.

"Hi." Cue awkward silence with a side of gawking.

"I didn't order any coffee." His admission has me envisioning my hands around Kate's throat. I feel my cheeks turn red.

"Oh, um…it's on the house—a 'welcome to Acton' coffee." *Could I sound any stupider?*

He glances at the cup with an amused expression, trying to gauge if I'm serious. He runs his right hand through his dark brown hair and reaches out with his left to grab the cup, gently bringing it to his lips to take a slow slip.

Maybe the slow-motion thing is just in my head, but nobody will ever know for sure. I don't even notice he's set it down and is staring at me.

When I finally come back to Earth, he reaches his hand out for mine. "Ethan."

"Aveline," I say, trying to pull myself together. He's just one guy, but for some reason he sets my nerves on edge.

"Aveline," he repeats, testing my name on his tongue. "Nice. You work here long?"

"Oh yeah, since it opened." I smile. "My mother is the owner."

"Ah, I see." When I realize he isn't going to offer me any information about himself, I decide I should get back to work.

"Well, nice to meet you. Enjoy your coffee." I sound like a complete moron. He mumbles a quick 'thanks' as I walk away.

I've never acted like that in front of a man before. It was like the power of his blue eyes put me in a trance and I couldn't control myself. Ignoring the urge to punish Kate for her trickery with a quick strangle to the neck, I go back to work on tomorrow's new recipe: buckeye brownie cupcakes.

*I really need to go to the gym.*

## CHAPTER TWO

*Ethan*

ACTON, COLORADO, IS a small town, much more so than I remember. When I heard the news that my Uncle Carl had passed, it felt like something in me settled. He was my last remaining relative, and it wasn't that I was happy he was gone, but it was like he was finally feeling peace. I don't know how I knew that, but it was something I felt in my gut.

I have to say, though, when I was told he left his house to me in his will, I wasn't all that surprised. We never really spent too much time bonding, but I was the only one in our family left, and really, it hurts me more than I'd tell anyone. I am officially all alone. Now there is no 'my family'.

The Marines are accommodating in these situations

and were willing to allow me leave, but I couldn't do it. I could not handle another funeral.

After my parents passed when I was a teenager, I felt like a part of me left this world with them. I was sent to live with Uncle Carl, whom I barely knew, on his farm in the smallest town in the universe.

It was a drastic change from my days in sunny California.

I loved being a Marine; it was my life, my passion. I live to serve, and I knew after joining it was what I was meant to do. After being in for six years, I wondered if there was something else—or rather *someone* else—I could invest my time into.

I haven't had a serious relationship since high school, and although that girl, Marie, said she'd do anything to be with me, military or not, I knew I had to break things off. I was only eighteen; I wasn't ready for marriage. Marie was going off to college anyway, and I knew she would meet someone else. Plus, I didn't love her.

Getting discharged forced me to start a new life. I've had it rough the last few months and am finally ready to get off my ass and figure out what I really want in life. Acton isn't going to be permanent, and I have every intention of going back to California. I want to go where the surroundings are familiar. I may have spent two years here in Colorado, but nothing about it feels like home, and I refuse to call it that.

Deciding I can't put off grocery shopping any longer, I start up Uncle Carl's old Ford pickup and make my way into town.

It's everything you'd expect out of a small Colorado town: miles of land covered with trees. I am happy to at least be living in the mountains; the farther east you go, the less appeal there is. At the very least, my time here will be spent surrounded by mountaintops. *Small blessings.*

Finally, about twenty miles later, I come into the small town, which is basically a main street lined with mom-and-pop shops with the bonus of a post office, bank, and library. It's Hallmark worthy.

I drive past a florist and a bakery, and there's also a gift shop, though I doubt many tourists come through here. The sight of the bakery makes my stomach growl with the realization that I slept through breakfast. I pull the old truck into a slanted parking space and climb out, getting a couple of stares from folks walking on the sidewalk, obviously wondering who the new stranger is. I give an older woman a nod and head for the bakery.

As soon as I pull open the door, the delicious aroma of the baked goods assaults my senses. It is the best smell I've ever smelled.

I walk to the counter to scour the many goodies in the display cases, and I notice a menu with different sandwich selections. I order my food and go take a seat to wait for it to be prepared.

I take my small paperback out of my back pocket to read but look up and get distracted by the beauty out the window. It is surreal to be back in this town, but it isn't a bad place to be. The people are decent, the views are amazing, and the mountains are a great perk.

Also, it isn't Afghanistan.

I'm lost in thoughts of mountain beauty and small-town life when I feel the eyes of someone staring. Lifting my head, I see a woman not much younger than me walking my way with a steaming mug in her hands.

She stares me down even as she stands next to the table studying me. I take the time to look her over as well.

Light brown hair is pulled loosely into a ponytail behind her head, and her eyes are the lightest green and familiar. She's not wearing any makeup, and somehow I know makeup won't change how pretty she is. She is naturally gorgeous all on her own.

Clearing my throat, I break her out of her daze.

"Hello."

Her eyes blink a few times before she replies, speaking so softly I almost can't hear her. "Hi."

"I didn't order any coffee."

She snaps her head over her shoulder, and the girl behind the counter tries to hide her laugh in a cough.

"Oh, um…it's on the house—a 'welcome to Acton' coffee." She's so flustered, and her cheeks turn red. It's cute.

I reach for the coffee and take a sip, trying to remember my manners.

When I reach my hand out, it takes her a moment to grasp it in return.

"Ethan."

"Aveline." *Damn.* It's then I know why she looks familiar. *Aveline Montgomery.* She's grown up since I last saw her, still as gorgeous as ever. She clears her throat, obviously uncomfortable.

"Aveline—nice. You work here long?" I hate small talk more than anything else, but she doesn't seem to remember me, and the last thing I want to do is ask if she remembers only to have her say she doesn't.

"Oh yeah, since it opened. My mother is the owner."

"Ah, I see." I quickly run out of things to say. It's strange that I struggle with talking to her—I'm not usually so flustered around women.

Our conversation comes to a standstill without either of us knowing where to take this. She fidgets with her fingers and gives me a small grin. Finally, she saves us both. "Well, nice to meet you. Enjoy your coffee." With that she turns and walks back behind the counter, quickly jabbing the other girl with her finger and disappearing behind the door.

After indulging in the best BLT of my life, I head down to the small market toward the end of the road where there is more parking. Grabbing a small basket, I start the search for food for the week.

I'm staring at a box of Pop-Tarts—a luxury for me—when I feel someone staring at me. It's something I've always been able to sense. Turning, I find Mrs. Mason with her eyes glued to me. She doesn't bother looking away when she notices that I see her, just waves and makes her way over.

I stifle a groan. I remember Mrs. Mason because she was always writing about me in her stupid paper, but I know better than to be rude to my elders.

"Ethan! Honey! It's been too long." She reaches out and hugs me, apparently oblivious to the concept of personal space as she squeezes me with all her might.

"Hi, Mrs. Mason. How have you been?" It's a courtesy question—I don't actually care about how she's been. Yes, I know I'm an asshole; no, I won't change. I like myself the way I am.

She launches into a long story about her husband and how Mr. Mason has some sort of fungus on his arm but his doctor can't figure out what's wrong with him and it's affecting her work on all her many committees and…really, I just don't care. In my head, I'm still contemplating if I want chocolate or strawberry Pop-Tarts, though I'm leaning strongly toward the latter.

"But anyway, I'm so sorry to see your Uncle Carl go. He was a good man."

The other part about moving back that sucks? This. This right here. Mrs. Mason is staring at me with sympathy in her eyes, but honestly, Uncle Carl wasn't that nice. He was a grump and kept to himself. Rarely did he ever even leave his farm unless it was absolutely necessary.

"I appreciate that. Listen, I gotta get going, but I'll see you around." *Because I'll be looking so I can run—or at least limp—in the other direction.*

"Oh sure, honey! See you real soon." She scoots her shopping cart around me and pats my shoulder. That's quite enough touching for one day. It's time to go home.

## CHAPTER THREE

*Ethan*

IT'S SNOWING, NOT that it isn't expected—I mean, it is April, and Colorado is known for spring storms. As I watch the snow fall, it's only about seventy percent regret I feel about my choice to wear flip-flops today.

I just finished my night history class at the local community college where I attend two nights a week, Monday and Thursday. The only trouble is they let out between nine and ten at night, meaning the snow has had plenty of time to pile up outside.

I really should consider checking the weather more often.

"Need a ride?" I look over my shoulder and see Pete, who is also in my history class. He's a cute guy with a surfer look. He doesn't really look like the type to be from Colorado, but I've known him almost my whole life.

"Nah, I've got my Jeep."

"All right, I know better than to fight you on it." He shakes his head, probably remembering all the times I've stood up for the vehicle. It was my dad's, and even though people can understand the sentiment, they aren't sure why I am still actually driving it. When I turned sixteen and got my license, my mother said I could have it, and I will always cherish it. It may be almost thirty years old, but I am never giving it up.

"Thanks anyway, Pete!" We both scurry out the door, the fresh snow falling steadily. Multiple students are all pulling out of the parking lot as I reach my car, and the cold of the snow has already numbed my toes clean through. I jump into the front seat and crank the engine, begging the heat to work this time—it tends to be picky on whether it wants to or not.

I'm near tears when it decides it is not going to work tonight. Fine, yes—I'm being dramatic. I reach into the back seat to grab my down coat to keep me warm. Home isn't exactly close to school, being about twenty miles up into the mountains.

I slowly pull out onto the road and start my journey. The roads aren't busy save for a couple other trucks and one plow that has started working its way in the opposite direction. I hoped that means he's already covered the road back to my house, but the odds of that aren't great. By the time I make it ten miles into the mountains, there isn't a single other car in sight. It isn't so bad though.

Snow is peaceful to me, almost like it is giving the earth a fresh drink to restart. The moon is peeking through the mountains and trees, reflecting off the white and making it feel like it is dawn. It's refreshing.

Just as I am about to pass the curve that leads into Old Carl's place, my back right side jolts to the left and suddenly I am spinning. I try to reason with the wheel, going with it and then releasing, but it doesn't seem to help a damn bit. My insides clench as I feel myself get thrown into my door, and suddenly everything just stops.

I'm breathing harder than I'd like to admit, and the sudden adrenaline is making my hands shake. I look around, wondering what the hell just happened. There is a very slim possibility that there is already ice on the ground; it's cold, but not cold enough for that.

Unclicking my seatbelt, I reach over for my phone and am not at all surprised that I have no cell service. Tilting my head back and letting out a heavy sigh, I contemplate my options: hike the remaining miles to the house in flip-flops or sit in my freezing Jeep.

Either choice will probably lead to some frostbite I'm not at all interested in having.

As I'm pondering my options, a sudden knock on the passenger side, which is facing the road, makes me jump out of my skin. I look over and see a big figure in a down jacket with the hood up raise a hand in greeting.

Seeing as I have no idea who this person is and he has a scarf wrapped around his face, I'm glad my doors are locked. I raise my hand and my eyebrows in question. He makes the gesture for me to roll down my window, and I shake my head and mouth 'no'—I may be desperate, but I'm not stupid. He does it again, and I shake my head again. He looks like he sighs, but then he finally unwraps his scarf and I widen my eyes in surprise—it's Ethan from the bakery.

I reach over the seat, thankful it's not a serial killer, and open the door for him. He jumps in to escape the cold and looks at me with an angry expression.

"What the hell are you doing?" His breathing is labored, and he looks like he's ready to kill me.

"Excuse me?" It's all I can think to say because...*what?*

"It's a blizzard out here and you're driving by yourself in this piece of shit Jeep?"

*Oh, I see.*

"First of all," I start, my finger in the air for extra emphasis. This dude thinks he knows best, and that just pisses me off. "I have lived here my whole life, so I know how to drive in the snow. Second of all"—another finger—"what does being alone have to do with anything? And third"—cue third and final finger—"do not talk shit about my Jeep."

He stares at me like I'm speaking gibberish and climbs out of the vehicle. Just when I think he's going to leave me to freeze to death, he grabs my book bag that contains everything I own, reaches over to grab my wrist, and yanks me across the seats.

"Hey! Wh—" Before I can finish my sentence, he has me hoisted up and over his shoulder like I'm a sack of flour. "Pardon me, sir," I say with a grunt as he starts trekking away from my car. "But what the hell do you think you're doing?"

He doesn't answer me, just keeps walking off the road and up a driveway. I can only assume it's Old Carl's driveway, and that's when I really start to panic.

Thoughts run through my head quickly: *Ethan is a stranger. Ethan is a stranger who is taking me to Old Carl's place. No one knows where I am, and I could potentially be getting kidnapped by a giant man with gorgeous eyes.*

Immediately, I start struggling, thrashing around to try to get out of his hold. He's strong but he's not expecting this and it throws him off balance, resulting in us both falling into the snow, me face first.

"Fuck," I hear him say, but I'm struggling through the powder, trying to get to my feet. Once I do, I take off running toward my car—at least if I get in there I can lock the doors and hope for someone in my family to come find me. Surely they're wondering where I am.

"Aveline! What the hell?" He is stalking toward me, not running, but seeing as I'm in flip-flops, he has the advantage.

"Stay away from me! I took self-defense!" I didn't, but I'm sure I could figure out some moves. I'm not paying enough attention and trip while trying to get away, consequently losing both my shoes, not that they were doing any good to begin with.

"Aveline, just stop, okay? I'm trying to help."

I look up from where I'm lying on the ground and see him standing over me with his hands facing out, presumably trying to seem non-threatening. His eyes seem sincere, but I can't help but smirk at him holding my purple book bag.

"Okay, fine. Freeze to death then—see if I care." He turns to leave, and suddenly my entire demeanor changes. I desperately don't want him to leave me there.

"Wait!" He stops and turns slightly, listening to what I have to say. "I'm sorry, okay? Please." I realize how pathetic I must look lying in the snow, completely at this man's mercy, but I'm out of options. I have no shoes, phone, wallet, or car, and I'm just praying he's a good person and I'm not walking into my death.

He walks right up to me, squats down, and lets out a deep breath. I see him leaning to one side in an awkward position, but before I can think much of it, he's hoisting me up bridal style and carrying me up the driveway.

It doesn't take long before I can see Old Carl's house. Unlike my grandparents' home, this one is a log cabin and has a cozier feel. I've never been this close to it before, and I'm seeing it now in a whole new light. It has been well taken care of and has the same style porch as our house, complete with its own rocking chairs. The lights make the house appear to glow from the outside, and the smoke rising out of the chimney indicates warmth I can't wait to get to burning on the inside.

Ethan walks through the door and after kicking it closed with his foot, he heads straight over to the fireplace. He sets me on the floor right in front of it then has me take off my jacket as he reaches to the back of the recliner and wraps an old quilt around my shoulders.

I watch as he proceeds to take off his own winter gear, throwing my bag on the small kitchen table. It's then that my brain finally catches up as to who he is.

"You're Old Carl's nephew, aren't you?"

He flinches and turns toward me, glowering. "Don't call him that."

"Sorry," I mumble. I'm curious as to why this bothers him so much; the man himself certainly didn't care too much. I've never seen this guy before, but part of Meryl's story was that Old Carl's—or I guess just Carl's—nephew lived with him for a few years during high school. I just never really did the math and didn't remember anything about that until now.

"Carl was my uncle though, so yeah." Ethan shuffles

into the kitchen and proceeds to fill a kettle with water before placing it onto the stove.

It's surreal being in Carl's house when I've never even so much as gone up the driveway. I stand from my place in front of the warm fire and browse the pictures above the mantel. Several show Carl in his prime with his arms wrapped around a young woman and a big smile on his face. I never once saw him smile like that; of course, I didn't spend a whole lot of quality time with him either.

Wondering who the woman is, I skim the rest of the photos, all of which are of him and this woman I'd guess was his wife some time ago. I reach the photo on the end, one of Carl standing next to a kid in his cap and gown. Neither of them are smiling, but you can tell they are related.

I feel Ethan walk up behind me and I turn. He hands me a warm mug, and once I accept it, he flops into one of the recliners with a heavy sigh.

"You went to high school here?"

"Yup." Maybe his curt answer is to stave off any more questions, but I can't help it. I am damn curious.

"How long did you live here?"

Another sigh leaves his lips before he answers, "Two years."

"How—" I'm interrupted by another deep sigh from Ethan. "What?"

"Are you gonna spend all damn night asking me questions?"

I open my mouth to ask him what crawled up his ass but then snap my mouth shut. "No."

Normally I wouldn't care, but for some reason I want Ethan to like me. Why? I have no idea. "I need to call my mom." I need to get out of here before I make a bigger fool of myself.

"Okay."

I walk to where he dumped my bag on his table and riffle through until I find my cell phone. Luckily, it still seems to be working. I quickly tap my mom's name on the screen and pray she isn't already in bed.

"Aveline?" My mother's worried tone comes across the line, and I breathe a sigh of relief.

"Hey Mom—"

"Where are you? You should have been home by now! I know you're an adult, but I'd at least like to know when you're going to be late—"

"Mom! Breathe, okay? My car spun out on the road and wouldn't start again. I guess I hit some ice or something."

"Your tire blew."

Startled by his words, I look up at Ethan, who's still sitting back in the recliner watching the fire.

"Aveline, who was that? Are you okay? Your brother was about to go look for you!" My mom takes a deep breath; she doesn't handle not knowing where her kids are well, which is understandable, but it makes me wonder how she'll handle me being in Europe alone.

"Mom, you need to calm down—you're going to hyperventilate. I spun off the road near Old—" I look up to see Ethan glaring at me. "Uh, sorry. I spun off the road by Carl's place down the road. His nephew is here and helped me get into his house. I'm okay but I need someone to come get me."

"What? No, it's not safe for anyone out there." I am surprised to hear that from Ethan and not my mom. Apparently, she can hear him, though, because she quickly agrees.

"Mother!" I turn my back to Ethan for a semblance of

privacy. "You expect me to stay here with him? He's a complete stranger!"

"Aveline, I'm sure it's fine. I remember him from all those years ago—heck, you were a sophomore when he was still in school." *Wait, what?* I have no memory of that whatsoever. How would I have not noticed him at school? Before I can ask any questions, my phone is ripped from my hand and Ethan is suddenly speaking with my mother.

"Hey! What the hell?" I glare at him, but he just stares at me.

"Mrs. Montgomery, I'd love to host your daughter until this storm blows over. We get pretty packed in here, as I'm sure you know, so she may not be able to get to work tomorrow." I can't hear what my mom is saying on the other end of the call, but whatever it is seems to please him because he smirks at me. "No problem. You enjoy your evening ma'am."

With that he hands the phone to me. I look at the screen and see that my mother already hung up.

*What in the hell just happened?*

Ethan shows me to a guest room that has a small, neatly made twin bed and some old Western-style pictures that look like they're glued to the walls. There's a small dresser across from the foot of the bed, a bedside table, and a lamp—that's it. I wonder what was in here before and conclude it had to have been Ethan's room.

The house is so small that I get the tour without even trying. Other than this room, there's one other, and it's the master, which is just a regular-sized room plus a bathroom down the hall. I already saw the kitchen and living room, and that's literally the whole house. It's not exactly sprawling, but the charm makes up for the lack of space.

I thank Ethan but he just nods and leaves me alone in the room. I guess we won't be swapping bedtime stories. With a sigh, I fall on the bed and try to sleep.

Awaking by slamming my face on the floor is not how I thought I'd start the day, but I temporarily forget where I am, including that I'm not in my queen bed at home. I stand and stretch, checking my phone for the time, and see it's already 6:30 AM. I haven't slept this late in a while; normally I wake up at 3:30 to head to the bakery.

I peek out the door and see the coast is clear; Ethan must be outside feeding the cows. It has to be in the teens outside, and I'm definitely not in any hurry to rush out into the cold; my feet are still freezing after last night.

Wandering into the kitchen, I see Ethan already made some nectar of the gods, AKA coffee, and I search for a mug. Filling it until there's just enough room for some cream, I stir in what I find in the refrigerator and look out the window to see if I can see anything. It's a whiteout, and I can't make out anything past about two feet.

My stomach growls and I put a hand to it. I wonder how prepared Ethan is for breakfast and if he would mind me snooping through his stuff. Guessing he probably wouldn't be too pleased but letting my stomach control my actions, I start rummaging through his pantry and fridge.

I find some ingredients to make some cinnamon rolls and get to work throwing everything together. It's so second nature to me now that I barely have to think about what goes into it. I learned to bake at a really young age;

my grandmother is excellent at it and passed her skills down to my mom, who always wanted a bakery. It's a family tradition, one I'm happy to be a part of.

Cinnamon rolls in the oven, I pour myself a second cup of coffee. As I'm pouring in cream, the front door opens and Ethan walks in, covered in snow. He's already discarded his boots on the covered porch and starts to unwind his scarf as he takes off his hat.

Without thinking, I make my way toward him to help him shrug out of his jacket, something I've helped my grandpa and dad and even Lucas with sometimes when the snow is plastered to their outerwear. I'm pulling it off his shoulders when I realize he's gone completely still. I stop and look into his stunned eyes then realize I basically just threw myself at him like some sort of fan girl. My eyes widen.

"I'm so sorry."

"It's okay." Ethan continues the job I started, and my face heats with embarrassment. I can't believe I just did that. I have no idea what got into me. He clears his threat and I glance up. "I'm going to go change really quick."

I nod my head and pick up the coffee cup, pretending to be fascinated with the creamer swirling inside it. I must be out of my damn mind—I just went right up to him and started stripping him like I was at a *Magic Mike* show.

By the time he shows his face again, I'm pulling the cinnamon rolls out of the oven, and the smell makes me smile. There's nothing like fresh baked rolls, and the cinnamon scent wafts through the tiny house. Ethan has walked up behind me, and I know this not because I see him, but because I can feel him there.

"Damn, I should have you over more often." I hold my

breath as he stands there. Not knowing what to say, I finally exhale with a forced laugh. I have no idea why he has me acting like a crazy person, but I can't freaking act normal around him.

"It's no big deal, just a thank you for letting me stay here." I finish frosting them and carefully serve one onto a plate. Ethan is sitting at the little table in the kitchen, sipping coffee, and as I hand him the cinnamon roll, he mumbles an expression of gratitude.

I return to grab one for myself and sit opposite him. It's uncomfortable for me; I hate sitting here in his house. I hate that I can't leave, but just by looking out the window I know I won't be leaving before noon.

We sit there eating in silence—well, he eats, and I mostly pick at my food, desperately wanting to apologize for being a spaz but not knowing if he even cares. He's hard to read; just when I think he's going to open up a little, he shuts down, like he wants to be tough about everything and doesn't want to reveal too much.

"Okay, I can't stand it." He raises an eyebrow at me with a mouth full of cinnamon roll. "I feel like an idiot—I shouldn't have touched you." Okay, I'm making this ten times worse. "Not like that," I rush on. "You know, just in general, like I shouldn't have tried to help you. I don't even know you."

He stares at me for a full minute like he's trying to figure out a science experiment. I fidget in my seat, not wanting to really look at him but unable to tear my eyes away. "It's no big deal." He gets up to put his dish in the sink, refills his coffee, turns toward me, and says, "Thank you for breakfast." Then he goes and sits in the chair he sat in last night.

I remain glued to my seat. I need to go home like yesterday.

"Are you serious?" I'm on the phone with my mom approximately five minutes after feeling dismissed by Ethan. "The roads are really that bad? What about the tractor?"

"Honey, have you looked outside? It's still snowing, and it's too dangerous." I walk to the window in the guest room I've escaped to, and sure enough, I can't even see that far out of the window because the snow is coming down too much. Damn Colorado spring weather. I let out a frustrated sigh and fall back onto the bed.

"Mom, he doesn't want me here. It's not an ideal situation." That's putting it mildly—I can't seem to stop embarrassing myself.

"It's just another day, maybe even this afternoon, but it's too soon to tell. Please just try to stick it out and be a good girl."

This is where the 'be a good little farm girl' mentality is kicked in. We were raised to be polite to every single person regardless of how they treat us, like the 'treat others how you want to be treated' saying, something my grandma says constantly. It's a good rule, sure, but sometimes it's just a pain in the ass.

"Fine. Call me when I'm released from prison."

"Aveline, I'm serious—you behave young lady." With that, she hangs up. *Thanks, Mom. Super duper.*

I'm debating whether or not I'm going to hole myself up in this room the whole time when I hear the recliner get let down and footsteps walking around. Putting on my big girl panties—which are the same ones from yesterday, *thank you very much*—I wander into the living room to see Ethan putting his jacket back on.

Farm work—I can do that. "Need any help?"

## CHAPTER FOUR

*Ethan*

I'M NOT THAT surprised Aveline wanted to help; she grew up doing this kind of work. The kids around here were raised on the idea that no one is lazy and every person pitches in. It's the work ethic I want to pass on to my future children—that is, if I ever have any. It's not looking like a possibility.

This storm kind of came out of nowhere, but it's not unusual to have a spring snowstorm like this in Colorado. It's why I have a love/hate relationship with this place. You never know what the weather is going to be like, and having a farm, the snow makes the work about ten times harder than it needs to be.

It's not the worst thing in the world having Aveline trail behind me as we walk the fence line to make sure none of the cows can walk over it. She keeps blabbering on about God knows what, and I impolitely continue to ignore whatever she's saying.

Don't get me wrong, Aveline is beautiful, and she's exactly what I would look for in a woman. However, it's been forever since I've been with someone, and I'm not looking for someone like her right now. The focus is to get the farm sold and move back out west.

Shaking the snow off the wire fence wasn't hard as it was pretty heavy and packed down hard. I reach back into the four-wheeler for the shovel when I'm hit in the back by what feels like twenty pounds of snow. Slowly I turn around and see Aveline covering her mouth with both hands, trying to hold in a laugh.

"You think that's funny?" Suddenly, she stops laughing and looks at me with big eyes. I reach down to grab a huge clump of snow.

"It was an accident, I swear!" But she's laughing again, and I don't really believe that. I launch the snow and it hits just above the galoshes she borrowed from me. It's the perfect spot to hit her because it falls into her boots, and her scream makes me laugh so hard my stomach hurts.

I walk over to see if she's okay, but her laughter tells me she's enjoying this. She's hunched over, and just when I think she's about to fall down, her arm comes up and smashes snow into the side of my head and down inside my jacket.

"Oh, ho ho, you'll pay for that!"

"I'll pay for that? There's ten tons of snow in my boots!"

Her laughter makes me smile, and I realize I haven't felt this light in years. Still, I can't take this lying down. I playfully tackle her back into the pile we made behind her, and she shrieks loudly as she grabs hold of my jacket, making me land straight on top of her.

This girl's laughter is contagious, and I can't keep my eyes off hers. They are lit with happiness, making the green irises shine. I notice I'm still lying on her and find myself not wanting to move. She doesn't show any sign of getting up either. Our eyes lock and she moves toward me, but before she can connect, I pull away.

"We'd better keep on." I pull her up and walk toward the four-wheeler. I know she's confused, maybe embarrassed, but I have to keep my head on straight when I'm around her.

We continue to work for a few hours and it goes by at a steady pace. She's a hard worker, which is something I can appreciate. She complains that I am too slow more than once and tells me it's a habit she got from her grandpa who was always throwing orders around.

We work in sync with each other and barely have to speak a word to get through most of the chores, something I am grateful for, and I'm guessing she is too after I rejected her kiss. We are working on the cows' water trough because the electric heater burned out and the water is frozen almost solid through.

"I hate these things." I unplug the heater from the wall inside the barn and grab two buckets. Aveline takes one from me without a word and starts toward the barn's wash sink to fill it with hot water.

I start to take the bucket from her when she pulls it back. I look at her, eyebrows raised.

"I can walk them out—you fill." She diverts her eyes down and walks around me to escape, but I reach out for her arm, which is hard to grab considering the jacket she wears engulfs her.

"You've been great, but I can carry them." Confusion gets the best of me. All of sudden she is acting shy, and I can't figure out why until her eyes land on my leg. "I'm fine," I say firmly.

"What happened?" It's a simple question with a painful answer, one I'm not ready to reveal.

"I don't want to talk about it." I grab the bucket from her and walk out of the barn to the cow pen, where I pour the hot water in the trough to begin the melting process.

I know I hurt Aveline's feelings, especially since we were goofing around earlier, but my story is mine. I told myself a long time ago I never want to share it with anyone, and that is my right after what I've been through. It's something that haunts me, not something I want to relive by telling the story over and over again.

I look up when I feel something hitting my cheeks. No, I'm not crying—it's snowing, again, which means Aveline isn't going anywhere any time soon.

We head in once we've gotten the cows some water and most of the chores are taken care of, at least the ones that are essential. We both hurry into the house to warm up and strip our outer layers then hang everything up. Aveline goes straight for the coffee pot and starts brewing some, and I head to the fire to add some wood. It starts to send out more heat within a couple minutes. I look to Aveline, who is rubbing her arms and doing a little dance by the coffee, and I realize she doesn't have clothes here.

I run into my room and grab some pajama pants and

a t-shirt, the best I can do for her right now. Walking back out, I see she's pouring some cream into her cup, and I'm surprised that I like seeing her feel at home.

"Here, you can borrow these." She stares at my outstretched hand for a beat. "You should take a shower and warm up. I'll make some lunch." She's looking at me like I grew a second head. I suppose my earlier reaction to her question may have spooked her, but I can't help that I don't like talking about my accident.

"Thanks." She snatches the clothes and practically sprints to the bathroom, where she closes the door. I hear the lock click into place a couple seconds later, like she hesitated in doing it. I can't blame her, though; it's not like we know each other.

I sigh when the thought that I don't want that to be the case crosses my mind. *Idiot.*

## CHAPTER FIVE

*Aveline*

MY BRAIN IS in a fog; I don't know what's wrong with me. What is it about being stranded here with Ethan that makes me act stupid? I've never acted this way, so clumsy and forward, and I've never tried to kiss someone I just met.

That was probably the most humiliating thing I've ever done. I watched his eyes, and I thought I knew what he wanted. It was so fun to not think about anything and just play; even though we were doing chores—which I normally hate—it was fun with Ethan. We chatted a little—okay, *I* chatted—and it was just so easy to work together.

Then I asked about his leg. I'd noticed before that he had

a limp, something I assume he got when he was a Marine, but I didn't think he'd have such a negative reaction to my question. He immediately shut down being friendly after I asked. He could have just said he didn't want to talk about it and left it at that, but no, he just went completely sour on me.

I was really surprised he thought about getting me clothes, but I was so grateful. I hate wearing clothes two days in a row, and even if I have to go commando, at least the pants are clean...and soft...and smell like him. I jerk my head up and look at myself in the mirror. *Oh my god, I was smelling Ethan's pants.*

I shake my head and throw the pants on the ground. I need to get a grip. Blasting the shower on hot, I begin to undress as I think about the events of the day.

He wanted to kiss me, I know he did—I've seen that look in guys' eyes before, though I usually turn them down. I've always hated dating, or the thought of dating. Whitney, who was my best friend all through high school, never had any problems dating, though. She dated half our high school, and she continued that way into college. Though we don't talk much anymore, I know there's little chance that's changed.

Nothing about it appealed to me though—the awkward silences, the *does he or doesn't he*, the fact that I have a slight anti-social problem. I did briefly go out with this guy, Jared, in high school. We went on a few dates, but I never wanted to go out; I preferred to sit at home and watch movies.

He hated that I didn't care. It was like he wanted me to be jealous of other girls, and he'd talk to them in front of me constantly. I only knew this because Whitney would always bitch about it for me, but I never even noticed.

Eventually, he broke it off. He acted like he was heartbroken, but I was left unaffected. He was not my cup of tea, and I honestly don't know why we 'dated'—if you can even call it that—for as long we did.

I let my mind wander under the hot spray, my body loving the chills it's giving me after being in the cold so long. I can't help but think of why Ethan reacts to things the way he does, like carrying a bucket. I know he has a leg injury and I've carried a million buckets in my life, so what was the big deal? Was he doing the guy thing, trying to show me he is tough?

Guys are complicated. I don't think I'll ever understand them, but now I understand why women want to fix them, because all I can think about is fixing Ethan.

※

Walking into the hall, I'm immediately hit with the smell of chili, and my mouth waters. Chili is the best winter food, even if it is technically spring right now. The kitchen is a mess as Ethan cooks away. It looks like the chili is already put together, but he's making sandwiches in the skillet.

It's fun to watch him in this kitchen. It's small, and I wonder how he manages to move. He hasn't noticed me standing in the door, and I take the time to admire him. He's still in his jeans from outside, but they're almost dry thanks to his coveralls. On top he's only wearing a fitted white t-shirt, and it shows off everything he earned in the military.

He spins around and slightly freezes when he see me,

and then he walks over and reaches his arm up toward my head. For a minute I think he's going to do something stupid (or incredibly smart, depending on your point of view), and it's only when he's really close that I realize my head is right by the cabinet that houses the plates.

"I made grilled cheese." It takes me a full minute to gather myself again, and he's already plating our food.

"I smell chili." *Captain Obvious gets a point.* "What's that for?"

"Dinner." He doesn't offer more, and I look out the window to see the snow has stopped falling. I don't say anything, not because I don't want to leave, but because he's already started lunch and it'd be rude to just leave now—at least that's the lie I tell myself.

---

Lunch goes over without any surprises, and I think I rein in my goofiness enough that he thinks I'm pleasant. After we eat, we sip coffee and watch the fire. He lets me borrow a book and we both read in silence. It's one of the nicest afternoons I've had in forever.

A while later we go back out to finish the evening chores. The cows don't seem interested in dinner enough to come out of their shed, but we throw feed anyway. He also has two horses in the barn that a neighbor was taking care of until he arrived. I didn't even think about the animals after Carl died, and I feel horrible at that realization.

It's finally time for dinner and I am starving, not to mention I was smelling chili all day and its aroma has invaded all my senses.

I grab myself a heaping bowl and sit at the table waiting for him (Ethan insisted I go first).

"I love chili," I declare as he takes a seat across from me, eyeing my bowl. I spoon a mouthful as he finally speaks up.

"Well, you've never had my chili—it's spicy and thick." Have you ever had chili come out of your nose? No? Well, it hurts like hell, and guess what, it's not a pretty sight.

"Oh god, are you okay?"

Ethan jumps up from where he was sitting while enjoying his food like a normal human being and runs to the sink to grab me a rag. I sit there with my hand covering my nose, completely mortified.

*I am never eating chili again.*

"Here." Ethan hands me a rag and stands like he wants to help, but man, how do you react in these situations?

"Um, yeah, I guess I was little caught off guard by what you said." My apology is cut off by headlights shining through the kitchen window. Ethan's brows furrow as he peers through it; he doesn't seem terribly concerned, but I get up to look too, because I'm nosy.

"Oh," I say when I see my brother jump out from the driver's side. It appears I've been rescued, and he couldn't have had better timing.

"Know him?" I think I detect a sharp tone, but I ignore it and explain that it's my brother. Ethan relaxes and heads to let him in the door.

"Thank God I made it!" Lucas is one of those people who is happy constantly, something he inherited from my dad but I didn't receive. "Hey man, I'm Lucas."

Ethan shakes his hand and stands back, clearly uncomfortable.

"Uh, wow! I didn't think I was getting saved today." I

regret the moment the words slip out; it sounds mean and isn't something I would have said if I had a filter. Ethan doesn't look at me. "I'll get my bag."

I skirt past them and rush to get my things—the three things I have, that is. I also grab all the clothes I borrowed and make a vow to wash and return them. Ethan and Lucas are discussing the weather, because what else is there to talk about?

"Ready to go?" Lucas hooks a thumb over his shoulder, tosses a 'see ya' to Ethan, and vanishes into the truck.

"Thank you, again, for the help." Ethan nods but doesn't say anything. "Seriously, you're practically my hero." My second attempt to get him to respond doesn't work either, and I take that as a sign that he's done with me and this conversation.

"All right, bye." I'm already to the top steps of the porch before Ethan says my name. I turn around to face him and see he's leaning against the door with one hand in his pocket, the other scratching the back of his head.

"I'll see you soon, okay?" It's a promise, and I narrow my eyes then nod. Walking to the truck, I wonder what exactly he means by that.

If only my eyes would stop watering. *Damn you, chili.*

# CHAPTER SIX

*Aveline*

THE MORNING CAME way too quickly today, and before I know it, I'm baking away at Mom's bakery. Unfortunately, I had to have my mom drop me off at the crack of dawn this morning while my brother rescues my poor Jeep today.

I feel exhausted; I didn't sleep well last night after Ethan dismissed me so easily. I know I said the wrong thing, but I just couldn't think fast enough.

I'm not usually intimidated by people, but Ethan is different. There's something about him that makes me want to impress him, and I know my day at his house didn't get the job done.

I'm lost working on the mint chocolate muffins that are on today's recipe list when my mom walks in the back door.

"Hey, hon." She's carrying more bags than any human should, and I glance at the clock: it's 9 AM.

"What are you doing back here so early? And what's with all the stuff?"

"Well, Sally and Meryl decided to throw a party at the old mill, and they asked me to make the desserts for it." She proceeds to pull random things out of the bags and throw them on my work surface.

"Hey! I'm working here!" I say in a Jersey accent—*it's excellent, trust me*. My mom seems to care very little about my work and continues what she's doing. "You never answered my question—what's with the early arrival?"

"Oh, I have so much to do!"

"Wait, when is this party?"

"Tonight."

"Tonight? What the heck? What is it for, anyway?"

"Ethan."

I whip my head toward my mother. She hasn't stopped organizing all her items, but what she said can't be right. I must have Ethan on the brain, which is not a good thing.

"What?"

"It's for Ethan." My mom finally stops and takes in my confused expression. "They want to welcome him home. He's been in hiding, and they want the town to get to welcome him back and thank him for his service."

I immediately think they couldn't have come up with a worse idea. There is no way Ethan would want to go to a party, let alone have one in his honor, and I tell my mother as much.

"Oh, I'm sure it will be fine. I do need your help, hon, with baking and serving." There's no way I want to go to this party. I don't even want to see Ethan ever again. *Lie.*

"Mom, I have school tonight." *No, I don't.*

"No, you don't." *Dammit.* My mom stops and looks at me, and I hurriedly turn the mixer back on. Unfortunately, it's not a loud one, so I can hear her just fine. "What's going on? Did you guys not get along or something?"

I sigh the way only a daughter can to her mother. "No, he was fine. It was me that was the problem. I need social skills lessons."

My mom cackles at me—yes, cackles. "Honey, I'm sure it was fine." With that she continues scurrying around, rearranging everything.

All I can think is, *Yes, I'm sure he already forgot I snorted chili.*

---

It's 11:30 AM and I'm about to fall over asleep. Mom has been busting my hide since she got here, trying to get all the desserts ready. Apparently this party is a big deal—upwards of three hundred people are supposed to attend. I'm pulling my tenth tray of cupcakes out of the oven when Kate comes running back.

"Aveline!" Her screech makes me jump even though I knew she was coming,

"What's wrong?" I should sound concerned, but my voice comes out monotone. I just don't have the energy.

"He's here." I don't have to ask who she's talking about; there's only one 'he' she could be referring to, but I try to play it off.

"So? You almost made me burn myself. Go take his order."

"Oh, I tried." I wait for her to finish but she just raises her eyebrow at me. I mirror her action. "He asked for you!" And the eyebrow was supposed to tell me this? I square my shoulders, readying myself for whatever Ethan could want, and walk into the front of the bakery.

He's standing there waiting patiently. It's hard for me to make eye contact, but I'm a freaking adult so I do it anyway.

"Hello." My voice comes out soft, and I clear my throat to try again.

"Hey." His voice sounds rough, like he hasn't talked all morning. Maybe he hasn't.

"So, can I get you something?" He quickly orders a sandwich, and Kate magically appears to fulfill the order. When he tries to pay, I wave him off.

"You fed me three times yesterday and housed me—please let me pay you back." He looks reluctant but puts his wallet away. He looks like he wants to say something, almost nervous, so I cut him off. "You excited for tonight?"

Ethan stares at me, completely confused.

"The party?" I fill in for him.

"What party?" *Oh no, they haven't even told him yet. Maybe it's supposed to be a surprise...?*

"Uh, well..." I'm trying to think of something good as an excuse and come up empty. Since it's Ethan I'm talking to, I decide to go with the truth. "The town is throwing you a welcome home party tonight."

He stares at me in shock and clenches his eyes, breathing deeply before pinning me in place with his piercing blue eyes. "Was this your idea?" He's clearly angry, and it's directed right at me. I hate it.

"No!" I scoff and give him a disgusted look. "It's the town, not me. I was hired to make food and serve—I'm not even a guest!" I don't know why I'm so mad, but something about him blaming me really pisses me off. Just as he opens his mouth, the bell on the door rings and Meryl and Sally hurry into the shop.

"Ethan! So good to see you again! Listen, we're throwing you a party tonight and we can't wait to catch up!"

"Mrs. Mason, that's very nice of you, but—"

"Oh, just wait until you see it! Well, why wait? Come with us! We'll show you everything!" Before Ethan or I can say any more, he's being physically dragged out of the bakery by both ladies. He shoots me one last look and I can't figure what it's supposed to say, so I just glare on instinct.

"Guess he's not gonna eat." I gasp and grab my chest, not having realized Kate was watching the whole scene. I look at the sandwich in her hand and grab it. It is lunchtime, and after all, I paid for it.

The end of this day can't come fast enough.

# CHAPTER SEVEN

*Ethan*

THIS CAN'T BE happening. A party in my honor is the last thing in the entire universe I would want. As I look at the old mill—which used to be the hookup place for high schoolers—I see this affair is much bigger than I expected.

There are white Christmas lights strung all over the ceiling—their attempt at "stars in the sky", according to Mrs. Mason. There are tables and chairs all over the place and, to my horror, a stage set up at the far end where a band is already setting up their instruments.

I can't believe this.

"Mrs. Mason, this really is too much—very unnecessary." I try my best to be polite to her, because even though

I'm past my boiling point, I know they really were just trying to be nice in the only way they know how.

"Ethan." She sighs and grasps my hands. This woman is way too touchy-feely. "Your uncle was important to the community"—*I know he would disagree*—"and I know you didn't live here long, but you're back now." Only temporarily, but I keep my mouth shut. "We want you to feel like you're a part of Acton, and plus, everyone is so proud of the young man you are."

I'm speechless, partly because they have no idea what kind of man I am, and partly because I've never seen Mrs. Mason actually be serious about something.

"All right," I say, because I'm obviously not getting out of this.

"Great!" She's back to her jolly self as she shoos me out of the building to "go get ready". I have no idea what that means, but I leave anyway and head home to…primp or whatever.

*Freaking idiot.*

Arriving at the party, I'm in shock—completely pissed off, mad as hell shock. There are maybe a hundred cars in the parking lot, making it so I have to park all the way up at the bakery for the second time that day just to go to this stupid thing.

I did change; my clean jeans and black button-up are as far as I'd ever go to 'dress up', and even at that I wish I was wearing a t-shirt and shorts.

This whole thing is making my mood sourer than ever.

Walking into the mill, I see people filling every corner of it. They're laughing and drinking, some are dancing, and others take pictures of the whole thing. It damn near looks like a wedding with the band playing in the background. Someone sees me and starts clapping, it spreads throughout the room, and I'm officially mortified.

People usher me in, moving me through the space faster than my leg can handle, and they clap me on the back as they shake my hand, thanking me for my service and giving me condolences for my loss. It's the oddest combination, and I'm not exactly sure what to say. *You're welcome, thank you* seems weird.

Finally, someone hands me a drink, and I take it gratefully. It's immediately half gone and then I'm shoved toward the food table. My temples seem to be sweating, either from the exertion of being rushed around on my bum leg or just having too many people around me.

Behind the table, near the baked goods is a sight for sore eyes. Aveline looks gorgeous; I can't even find it in my Grinch heart to deny it. She's wearing a black dress I think hits at her knees, though it's hard to see through the crowd, and her hair is down, flowing and beautiful. She has makeup on, which she doesn't need, but it just enhances her beauty, and she looks like a cover model. *Geez, when did I start thinking girly shit like that?* I make eye contact with her, and she immediately loses her smile and looks away.

I can't say I'm not ashamed by how much of an asshole I was yesterday. She doesn't understand why I reacted the way I did, but that's not her fault.

Today, I went into the bakery to apologize, and not only that, I was working up the nerve to invite her to dinner. When I got there, though, my stomach clenched with nerves, and before I could ask her, she sprang the party on me, instantly pissing me off.

As I approach her, I lose my balance a little and lean on the table. Aveline reaches forward like she's going to catch me, and I look in her eyes as I see her eyebrows scrunch with worry.

"Hey." She starts walking toward me from behind the table and grasps my elbow. "You okay?"

I nod my head and stand at full attention, putting me a few inches above her. She's still looking at me like I've got red eyes and horns.

"Excuse us a minute," she says to the group that's been hounding me for over an hour. Then she nods at her mom.

We walk out of the main entrance and I let her lead me around the side where there's more privacy. I didn't realize how sweaty I was until walking outside, and I take a deep grateful breath of the fresh air.

"Thank you." I look at Aveline and, if possible, the moonlight makes her more beautiful. *I'm screwed.*

"No problem. You looked like you were about to pass out. Let's sit." She motions toward the ground and I grin, loving that she doesn't care that the ground is wet and she's wearing a dress.

"Ground's wet."

She scoffs. "I couldn't care less. I've been on my feet for forever, and you look like you could use a bend in the legs." The saying cracks me up because it's something my uncle used to say when he was tired. "What?" She looks at me like she's embarrassed.

"Nothing."

We sit next to each other in the silence, the music muffled by the wall that separates us from it, and I exhale a huge sigh.

"I could tell you were suffering the minute you walked in the door." She grins like she's teasing me, or maybe she's happy I was miserable; it's hard to tell.

"Yeah, crowds aren't really my thing."

"Me either."

I look at her and study her profile. I'm a sucker for her lips, and I wish I hadn't acted like an idiot earlier.

"What is your thing then?" I ask.

She pauses before she gives her answer, looking down at her hands where she's twisting them together.

"Travel."

"Travel?" It's not what I was expecting.

"Well, maybe."

"I don't get it."

She looks embarrassed, and I wonder if this is the first time she's admitted this to someone.

"I want to travel." She finally meets my eyes, attempting to see if I'm going to make fun of her or something. "I've been saving money forever, and that's the goal."

"That's..." I search for a word. "Admirable."

"Really?" She sounds genuinely surprised by my reply, and I wish so much that I wasn't a huge asshole.

"Yeah. I mean, you want to travel, you should travel." Myself, being a Marine, I've been all over the world. I just never went to tourist destinations, more like war zones and camps.

"Thanks." She smiles. "I think I will." I laugh with her and we settle into the silence.

"You know, I remember you." Aveline's green eyes widen in surprise at my statement, and I kind of wish I'd kept my mouth shut.

"You do? Really?" Genuine surprise laces her voice.

"Yeah, from school. You were just about the shiest girl in the whole place. You always had your nose in a book—it was cute."

"I don't get it! I do not remember you, but I feel like I should."

I scratch my jaw, embarrassment creeping up on me about how bad a guy I was in high school. I'm an asshole now, but back then I was an even bigger one, and worse, it was to hurt people.

"I'm glad you don't. I wasn't a good guy back then."

"But you are now?"

Considering her question for a minute, I make a move and reach out to grasp her hand with mine. "I think I'd like to be."

She smiles at me, and I feel like I've won the lottery.

# CHAPTER EIGHT

*Aveline*

THE REST OF the night keeps on at a steady pace. This little town loves to throw parties, and I think this may be the biggest one we've had in years, other than our annual Thanksgiving dinner. Ethan is completely out of his element and hates every minute of it, but he takes it in stride.

I'm absolutely blown away by our conversation earlier. I can't wipe this grin off my mug for anything in the world, not even when my mom starts making fun of me for being "swept off my feet". Staring at the dancers who are swaying to a slow song out on the floor, I sway back and forth behind the dessert table.

"Oh my, my girl's got it bad." My mom grins and I nudge her shoulder.

"Stop, I'm just having a nice time."
"Uh huh, sure."

I just keep smiling, and it gets even bigger when I see Ethan making his way over to my table. He's got a small smirk on his face as he walks to the end of the table where I can meet him. The song switches to another slow song, and he holds his hands out to me.

"May I?"

I don't even bother looking at my mother to make sure she's got the table because honestly, I don't really care. I take his hands immediately and follow him out. Hoping and praying my clumsiness is behind me, I step into his arms and let him lead. We go slow, and it's the happiest I've been in forever.

"This isn't so bad," I say as he looks down at me. "I'm a lucky girl—I think I'm the only one you've danced with tonight."

"Ah, actually, you missed it: Mrs. Mason already staked her claim."

Giving him a face, I laugh. "Guess I've got some competition, huh?"

We laugh at the thought and continue to spin. When Ethan decides to act pleasant, he's not so bad. Enjoying a dance with someone is new; I wasn't a fan of high school dances, so this is a first for me. When the song ends, we leave the dance floor and walk to get a drink.

The party is winding down and people are leaving quickly. I see they're packing up the food, and I realize my time with Ethan tonight is over.

"Guess I'd better get back to work. Looks like you're officially off the hook."

He lets out a long sigh and smiles a little. "Thank God. It

was a long night, but not as horrible as I imagined it would be." He gives me a look like I had something to do with it, and I grin so big I think I probably look like the Joker.

"Well, I'll see you soon?" It comes out as a question, though I didn't intend it to.

"Aveline, part of the reason I was coming to see you this morning was..." He pauses and takes a deep breath like he's about to tell me he's dying. *Oh no, please don't tell me you're dying.* "I was wondering if you'd like to have dinner with me."

*Oh, well, good—not death, just asking me out.*

"Oh, uh, yeah."

"Cool." He grins and grabs my hand to give it a squeeze. "Tomorrow?"

"Tomorrow."

We say our goodbyes and I get back to work packing up the dessert table to take it all back up to the bakery.

I have a date with Ethan tomorrow.

*Oh shit—I have a date with Ethan tomorrow.*

⛰⛰⛰

Wednesday morning after the party, I wake slowly, the wetness of a dog's nose rubbing against my arm. I absentmindedly rub Stud's head, the big Bernese Mountain Dog needy for attention as usual.

It's one of the few days off I normally take from working at the bakery. My mind immediately goes to the day ahead, and my eyes pop open at the realization that today is my date with Ethan.

Normally, dates don't faze me. If they work out, great,

cool, but if not, great, whatever. I just don't typically care. This date, though, I care about. I don't know what it is about Ethan or why I care that he likes me, but I do.

I care a lot.

He's kind of a mystery. At our first meeting, I thought he was a total asshole—which he is—but these last few encounters we've had—him talking to me outside the mill, us slow dancing at his party—have made me see him in a whole new light, and I think I like him.

I rise from my bed, reaching high, and throw my arms behind me, completing the stretch, the best part of the morning. Wandering down the stairs, I find my grandparents sitting at their breakfast table and seek out my nectar. Once I've settled down at the table with them, my grandmother pushes the muffins she's made to my side of the table. The baking gene is very strong in my family.

It's just us in the house this morning. My brother is at school (he's a senior this year) and Mom's already been at the bakery for hours.

"Any plans today, Avie?" My grandma has called me Avie since I was a young girl and it drives my mom nuts, but I love the term of endearment.

"Oh, not much," I reply while picking at a muffin. Tossing some under the table for Stud, I ignore the stink eye my grandma gives me.

I'm not sure how much I should share with them about my date with Ethan. Truth is, the fact that we danced at the party has probably already spread around town.

"Really?" She peers at me over the edge of her newspaper, her eyes all knowing and full of the same expression she's used on Lucas and me since we were children.

"Nope." I make sure to pop the P sound and reach over

to read a discarded section of newspaper.

She hums at me and just when I think she's dropped the subject, she speaks up again. "So, how was that party last night?"

"Weren't you there?" I distinctly remember her chatting shamelessly with Meryl and Sally last night. She's a hopeless gossip herself, even though she'd never admit to it.

"Well, we left early, but there's some gossip we've heard about something that happened after we left."

See, I knew word would have spread already. People really need to get out of town more often. She pushes over another section of the paper and right there on the front page is a huge blown-up picture. It's grainy, but the subjects are very clear: Ethan and me, slow dancing.

I sigh and let down my defenses. There's no point now that the entire town and probably everyone in the surrounding two hundred miles knows we danced.

"All right, let me have it."

Grandma takes a giant breath and launches into her spiel about why this is such a horrid idea. "He's not the kind of boy you get involved with." She would probably say this about any boy I dated; she hated Jared. "You must remember what a little charmer that boy was when you were in high school. He had a different girl every time I saw him and left that poor little Marie to fend for herself."

"Ugh! Why does everyone remember him but me?" I throw my hands in the air for emphasis. Grabbing my now empty mug, I make my way over to set it in the sink.

"Leave her alone, Sandy," Grandpa says without looking up from his paper. I grin in his direction and then at Grandma, who gives me puppy dog eyes.

"I just want you to be careful, that's all." Her tone is sad and immediately makes me feel bad.

"I will be, Gram." I walk behind her to wrap her in a hug around her shoulders.

"I want to reintroduce myself to him before you leave, so no running out the door."

"Um, I think we'll probably meet somewhere." Yes, that will be much better than my entire family staring him down when he picks me up. The Spanish Inquisition will not be recreated here tonight, no sir.

"No ma'am. A gentleman picks up a lady for a date." Grandpa *mmhmms* in my direction, and I release a breath again.

"All right, I've got to run some errands." I make my exit and rush upstairs for clothes. Deciding I need a new outfit for this date, I dress in jeans and tennis shoes so I'll be comfortable while I shop. I opt to leave my face bare and rush out the door before I can get deterred again. If I'm not careful, I'll end up on a double date with my grandparents.

I stare at myself in the long mirror that leans against the wall in my room. I can't stop fidgeting with my shirt, not sure if it's too clingy or revealing. Ethan texted me earlier—apparently he stole my number while I was his house guest a few days ago—saying he'd pick me up at 5:30.

It's now 5:25, and I can't seem to keep my palms dry. These nerves are something completely new, and I'm not sure how I'm supposed to handle the swimming pools that are my hands right now.

As I'm contemplating stuffing some tissues under my

armpits to keep them dry, our old doorbell rings. My heart rate kicks up and I quickly grab my purse before rushing to the door, but my hopes to be the first one there are dashed when I hear Lucas welcome Ethan in like they're best friends.

He's surrounded by my family before I even get down the last of the stairs, and he's busy trying to answer the question my grandma directs at him when he finally looks up and sees me. I feel my stomach lodged tightly in my throat at the smile he sends my way. God, he has the most gorgeous smile.

"Okay guys, give him some room to breathe." I basically have to peel my relatives off of him before lightly nudging him back toward the door—they somehow pulled him ten feet into the foyer within seconds. I snatch my jacket but before I can throw it on, Ethan grabs it from my hands and helps me into it. It's such a sweet thing to do, and I can hear my mom sigh from behind him.

"Have her back before dawn, son," my grandpa calls out, and Mom and I both scold him at the same time. My cheeks burn and now I'm completely mortified along with being out-of-my-mind nervous.

Ethan chuckles and says, "Yes, sir."

"Oh my god." I groan and whip the front door open before practically jumping down the stairs. I slow when I realize Ethan is taking his time, a smile firmly in place.

When we reach the passenger side of his truck, I finally face him. "I'm so embarrassed."

He chuckles good-naturedly. "It's all right, I thought it was pretty funny."

He opens my door and I look back at the house to see four faces plastered to the front window. Groaning again,

I jump into the truck. Ethan glances back to where I was looking and full-out belly laughs. If I wasn't so damn embarrassed by my crazy family, I think I'd enjoy this moment.

*Thank you, dear family, for ruining my moment.*

# CHAPTER NINE

*Ethan*

NEVER IN MY life did I think I would be so grateful to date a girl with her family so up in her business. My nerves were on high alert on the drive over to pick Aveline up. There's something about her that makes me want to not be an asshole, and for some reason, that makes me act like a woman. I was sweating and fanning my face to keep my cool before I got there.

As soon as her brother opened the door, questions were thrown at me. I get why they're worried; her grandparents remember me from back in the day, and her mom once had to scold me during a homecoming dance she was chaperoning, a story I doubt Aveline has ever heard.

The second I saw Aveline, though, my breathing evened

out. Something about her seemed to calm me down, and it wasn't a feeling I can say I've ever experienced. She is dressed in jeans with boots that reach almost to her knees and a blue blouse. She looks nervous but is glowing. Her simple outfit and the fact that she isn't trying too hard for me make me like her even more.

Now, she is sitting in my passenger seat, fidgeting with her hands in her lap, something I've noticed her doing whenever she's around me. Somehow, her being nervous makes me not be anymore.

"You okay?" I ask as I get onto the main stretch of highway that is basically the only road to get to either of our houses.

She turns her green eyes on me. "Who? Me? Yeah, totally!" She squeaks at the end and I mash my lips together to hold in a laugh. Aveline is the most awkward girl I've ever met and the only person that can make it endearing.

"Okay. How was your day?"

"Oh fine, yeah." She pauses and then opens her mouth like she forgot something. "How was yours?"

She's staring at me, and I chuckle a little. "It's going pretty great." I grin at her with a smile I used to make the girls swoon in high school, and the effect clearly works because she just stares at my face like I'm a ghost.

"Um…" She pauses and readjusts in her seat to face the windshield. "Where are we headed?"

We're still on the highway but when we come to the fork, I turn away from Acton. "I thought we could go somewhere where not everyone knows us, maybe get some privacy."

Her cheeks redden, and I wonder how innocent she really is. Then, I think it's probably not a thought I should allow to linger in my mind just yet.

We continue the drive in silence and enjoy the scenery passing quickly on each side of us. It's easy to ride through the mountains in silence with everything there is to look at. The quiet isn't uncomfortable for me, though something I'm not generally very good at is sitting with another person without talking to them.

We pull into the town that's almost a replica of Acton, just with a different name and a huge perk: a steak house.

"Steak?" Her eyes light up when I pull into the parking lot and turn off the gas. I don't answer her, just rush out of the door. I'm slower than the average human, but thankfully, she waits in her seat for me to open her door. I help her down and grasp her hand before she has a chance to outwalk me.

"I hope that's okay. I've been craving one, and as good as your sandwiches are, steak is one of a kind."

"Not to worry, I'm not offended—I don't make the sandwiches."

"Oh?"

"Nah, we have a cook in the back, and she is pretty amazing."

We enter the steakhouse and the smell immediately makes my mouth water. I look at Aveline and can tell she's on the same page. We get seated right away and order shortly after. While the food is prepared, I try to think of things to talk about. Unfortunately, I'm terrible at it.

We sit in silence for a bit. She starts fidgeting with her hands again, and I can't take it anymore.

"Why do you do that?" My question comes out harsh. I didn't mean it to, but, well, it's out there.

She looks at her hands and diverts her eyes to one of

the TVs on the wall behind me. "You make me nervous."

"Why do I make you nervous?" Could be because I'm a dick, but I'll let her answer this one.

"I think it's because you seem to change your mind about me a lot."

I sigh and run my hand through my short hair. She's right; in the first encounter we had, I wasn't exactly nice, and then the next day, I asked her out.

*Maybe I'm bipolar.* It wouldn't surprise me.

"I'm sorry. I'm just trying to do the right thing."

"Who says there's a wrong thing?"

I smile at her reasoning. She's right, of course—there is no real reason we couldn't work, except I'm not staying here, and neither is she. I push the thought away and she starts talking again.

"So, how's it feel to be back here?"

I consider her question before I answer. "It's different. I'm a different person than I was in high school."

"I can appreciate that. I still can't believe I don't remember you."

I grin, thinking about how nerdy she was. "It's probably because you never took your nose out of a book."

She laughs, and it's the best sound. "Yeah, could be." Her eyes roam over my face and she shakes her head like I'm not real. "Um, did you play any sports or anything?" she asks.

"Nah, I was a different kind of player."

Based on her facial expression, I've stunned her. "Oh."

*Wow, nice one, Ethan. One sentence and you've ruined this date. Check please.* "Just kidding, I played some football."

"Well, I didn't really date much. Guys didn't like me."

The fact that she's basically ignoring how I could have ruined this makes me happy, and I turn the conversation onto her.

"Yeah?"

"Yeah, I had one serious boyfriend—well, 'serious' is a loose term." She rolls her eyes. "He didn't enjoy me much."

I scrunch my eyes together. "Why not?" I can't fathom how that's possible.

"Well, he liked showing me off, and I didn't care for it. I'm content with being home."

"That and traveling don't usually go hand in hand, ya know." I smirk at her to show I'm teasing.

"Gee, didn't think about that." She touches her lips with her index finger and my attention sticks there. "Guess I'll have to change my whole plan." She giggles, and I train my eyes back to hers.

The food gets delivered and I'm relieved that she eats as quickly as me. We banter back and forth while we eat, and it's the easiest date I've ever been on—one of the most fun, too. When the food gets cleared, I pay the check and then grab her hand, pulling her up.

"Thank you for dinner," she says as we step outside.

The sun is long gone, but I'm not quite ready to say good night yet. "Walk with me?" She nods her head like she knew the question was coming.

We stroll down the street, just window shopping since the small shops have been closed for an hour or so now. It's easy and I'm completely content with her by my side. It's been a long time since I could just hang out with someone without being uncomfortable.

It's then I realize us going our separate ways might hurt a little when the time comes, which, inevitably, it will.

"Ethan?" I turn to look behind me because that voice

wasn't Aveline's, and my stomach drops a little at the sight in front of me.

"Marie." It's my high school girlfriend, the one who was in love with me, the one I didn't love back, the one I dumped when I left for the Marines.

"Wow," she says, stepping toward me with her arms wide, nearly knocking Aveline in the face. I grip her hand, but she has to move her head to get out of the way. I don't return the hug.

"It's been a while, huh?" She steps back only half a step so we're breathing the same air. I take my own step back—or maybe two or three—dragging Aveline with me.

"Yup. This is Aveline." I gesture toward her even though this encounter is insignificant and she doesn't need to know Marie.

"Uh huh. So, wow, you're back." She's not very smart. "We should catch up sometime."

"Okay, we gotta go." Not wasting another second of our date, we head toward where the truck is parked, leaving Marie standing there with her mouth gaping.

"Sorry," I say softly.

"It's fine." Aveline stays quiet for a minute, and I wonder what she's thinking. Obviously, that was weird, but it won't be the end of our date.

Once we're settled back in the truck, I turn it over and turn the heat on low. The snow has mostly melted due to Colorado's weird weather—it's been sixty degrees for two days now. I turn my head in her direction and try to assess what's going on in her mind.

"So..." She starts, looking at me with a little grin. "Ex-girlfriend?"

"Very ex. It's really surprising you don't remember people from high school. It's like the smallest high school in the world."

"I was in my own world," she mumbles, and I think I've embarrassed her. I grab her hand and pull her toward me, and then I tuck her hand under my arm and caress her cheek so she's looking at me.

"That's okay, but know that no other girls are present in my world right now." I stare at her eyes and she latches onto mine.

I take my opportunity, this time not letting the moment pass by. I press my lips to hers and she responds immediately, grabbing my forearm, holding my arm there. Nudging her lips open, I slip my tongue against hers, and we fight for dominance for a moment.

It's not the first time I've kissed a girl in this truck, so it shouldn't feel like this. I shouldn't have goose bumps, shouldn't be holding her head hostage so she can't back away, and I really shouldn't want it to never end.

*Shit.*

# CHAPTER TEN

*Aveline*

I'M FLOATING. THE clouds have lifted me to the skies and nothing can touch me. I have no stress, no worries. I am light as a feather.

No, I'm not dreaming. This is how I feel as I watch the mixer stir the batter around and around, my brain stuck in the love bubble that was created last night. I'm so completely lost in my fantasy world I'm not expecting it when Kate says my name—right next to my ear.

It makes me jump and knock into the mixer, and my hand hits the button that puts it on full speed. The action happens so quickly neither Kate nor I can stop it and batter splatters everywhere, all over my apron, which started out clean. It's in our hair and our faces, on the counter and the floor.

Finally, I manage to turn the whole thing off by ripping the plug out of the outlet.

We stand there staring at the mixer and its destruction. As if directed in a movie, we look at each other, and the second I get my eyes on Kate, I can't help but laugh at her. She's completely covered in batter, and I'm sure I don't look any better.

"Oh my god! What on earth?" she screeches, but as soon as she touches her hair and feels the wetness, she can't help but giggle.

"Sorry," I say, not even sure where to start.

"I'm sorry! I can't believe I scared you so bad." She looks me in the eyes and squints like she's trying to read my thoughts. "What was going on in there?" Tapping my head, she comes away with batter on her hand, and then she finds us some hand towels to attempt to clean up.

"Nothing, sorry, in my own world."

"You know, you shouldn't try to hide it—I know you had a date last night." Of course she does. The whole world knows like it was on *Good Morning America* this morning or something.

I blush and start to wipe myself off before starting the cleanup of the kitchen. Last night will never be topped; I've convinced myself of this fact. Even if I got kissed on the moon, it couldn't beat what I felt last night.

So, it's been a while since I've dated, sure. However, this feeling with Ethan was undeniably intense. My lips tingle at the thought of his, and I wonder when I'll see him next. He dropped me off just before eleven after we spent some more time in his truck. We didn't do more than kiss, but it was the best date of my life.

"Well?"

Kate's prodding is only the first of many, I'm sure, but I don't even want to share the details. They're mine. I want to lock them in a chest and stuff it under my bed for safekeeping.

"It was nice."

"Uh huh, that's not really a 'it's nice' face. That's more like a 'God, I can't wait to have his hands on me again' face," she says with a straight face, and I can't help but gape at her.

"Kate! That's so inappropriate!"

She shrugs, unbothered. "So? I want details."

"There's nothing to share." Kate glares, but I don't budge.

"Fine. I'm gonna clean myself up."

She twirls like a dancer and flits out of the room to go to the bathroom in the front of the store, and I turn back to the mess in front of me. I can't stop thinking about Ethan, and as amazing as it is, it still scares me a bit. I'm still planning my trip, but now it seems less important, or maybe just not something I need to rush off to.

Pushing that thought aside, I finish cleaning and keep my morning tasks going, finishing the muffins we made the special for the week and setting them on the trays to be taken out to the front. Finding the flow of the baking and following the recipes finally allows me to get my work done in time to get a few hours of rest before my class tonight.

All I want to do is see Ethan. *I'm in big trouble.*

Class is boring as usual. Getting a general business degree doesn't exactly speak to my passions per se, but I don't need to learn how to bake, and learning how to keep the business going in the future will be a good asset for me to have.

My English class, however, is one of my least favorites, and the professor drones on and on for a good three hours before finally releasing us. What I learned: I need a haircut. I mostly stared at my hair the entire time as I fiddled with it while the teacher talked.

"Aveline!" I turn around as I'm walking down the hall to head to the front doors and see Pete rushing toward me. He bumps into a couple, and they don't seem happy to have been disturbed.

I smile as he gets near me then laugh a little as he trips over his feet and almost falls.

"You okay, Pete?"

"Yeah, hey." He's breathless once he's standing in front of me, my beauty obviously taking his breath away. *I'm hilarious.*

"What's up?"

He smiles at me and runs his hand over his hair, trying to fix the strays. "I was wondering if you'd like to have dinner sometime?" Pete's smile turns a little unsure, and I get that pit of guilt in my stomach.

Let me just clarify something here: I'm the worst at saying no. I hate letting people down and hurting their feelings—it's the worst thing in the world, and seeing Pete's nervous yet hopeful smile makes it a thousand times worse.

"Oh..." I stall and try to think about how to let him down easy. "I'm sorry, I'm kind of seeing someone." At least I hope I am.

"Ah, dang." He looks like he kind of expected it but also kind of like I kicked his puppy. I'm a horrible person. "That's all right."

"I'm sorry." I hope he sees my sincerity.

"It's fine, really." He opens his arms for a friendly hug, and I can't deny him that. After a quick embrace, we step out the front doors and start on our separate ways.

When I round my Jeep and see a figure leaning against the side, I gasp and clutch my chest. "Oh shit!" I squeak. When the person steps out and I see it's Ethan, my heart rate starts to slow, but only a little. Who hides behind a car at ten o'clock at night?

"What the hell are you doing here?" As scared as I was, I also can't deny that I'm happy to see him.

"Who was that?" It's then I notice the slight glow of an ember coming from his right hand.

I squint at him. "You smoke?"

He looks at his hand like he forgot he was even holding it and quickly puts it out. "Who was that?" he repeats, and it takes me a second to register it in my brain, still clutching my chest and processing the fact that not only is Ethan here, he was smoking.

"Uh, who? Inside?"

"Yes, Aveline." His tone is like someone talking to a toddler, and while I'm annoyed, I also want to laugh at the face he's making.

"That was Pete. We went to school together—I've known him forever." His eyes narrow, but I press on. "What are you doing here?"

He shrugs and gestures toward my car. "I figured you were driving this piece of junk and probably needed a safe way to get home."

The happy feeling disappears. I know it may be an old car, and yes, it has a ton of miles on it, but it was my dad's, and despite it being childish, it pisses me off when people make fun of my Jeep.

"Well, you've wasted your time." I push past him and try desperately not to breathe in his masculine cologne. *Damn, why does he have to smell so good?*

"Hey, seriously." He reaches out and grabs my bicep to turn me. I look at him with steely eyes—at least that's what I try to do. "It's not safe, let me drive you."

"I'm fine, Ethan. I don't need a ride." He takes a deep breath, and I wonder if he's ever had a woman argue with him before.

"Please, Aveline." His eyes! They do me in. What is it with blue-eyed boys? They just automatically make women swoon—so unfair.

I stand up as straight as possible and look him in his gorgeous swoony eyes. "Say you're sorry."

He blinks. "Sorry? For what?"

"For insulting my car." I don't give him a reason, not because it's something that's hard to explain, but because I want to see if he'll do it.

"Okay, I'm sorry. I didn't mean to offend you." He seems sincere enough, so I allow—yes, allow—him to lead me to his truck. Like a gentleman, he opens my door and helps me up. After he shuts the door, I can't keep the grin off my face.

I don't have the talent to wipe it away before he's in the driver's seat and turning the truck over.

Ethan glances my way and smiles. "What's with the grin?"

I shrug, slightly embarrassed to be so happy just to see

another human, which is not my usual reason for being happy. "I can't believe you picked me up."

He sighs, but he's not annoyed, more like uneasy to admit what he did. "I didn't wanna have to haul you off the side of the road again."

I gasp and stare at him, and he just smirks over at me as he gets onto the highway. "You jerk!" I nudge his arm.

I don't think I've ever been giddy in my life, but I think that's what this feeling is. I also think I'm supremely enjoying it.

# CHAPTER ELEVEN

*Ethan*

I PUT NO conscious thought into picking Aveline up. I was enjoying a book by the fireplace, worn out from a day of fixing up the farm and sorting old junk to get the place ready for potential buyers when I remembered she had class tonight.

Pushing Aveline out from my thoughts wasn't an easy task today. Last night was better than I could have hoped for, but I didn't want to be some poor sap who sat around thinking about her all day, so I threw myself into work until my leg couldn't take it anymore.

I wanted to see her again tonight but knew she was in class so I didn't even text her. Then, thinking about how out of the dating scene I've been, I realized not talking to her all day was probably a bad move. All of this took place within the span of five minutes.

Without questioning it, I was out the door, in my truck, and driving to the only local community college Acton has. The campus isn't even in Acton, but it's the best we have around here.

Not knowing what time her class got out, I got there around 9:30. I was relieved to see her old Jeep still in the lot and parked my truck next to it.

Just after ten, I hopped out of the truck, ready to intercept her, and I saw her stop in the lobby to look behind her. A guy who looked to be about our age ran toward her, almost falling over himself. His stance made me nervous and, out of habit—a bad one I am trying to break—I lit up a cigarette.

I could clearly see Aveline from where I stood and saw her shake her head a little. The guy's head bowed, and she reached out to give him a hug. I've never been a jealous kind of guy, but the sight made my blood boil.

Taking an angry drag of my cigarette, I walk to the back end of her Jeep, just behind the back door, and lean against it, out of view. When she comes around the corner, she gasps and clutches her chest.

"Oh shit!"

I don't even have it in me to smile at how easily I scared her.

"What the hell are you doing here?" she asks with a light tone like she's hiding that she's happy to see me.

"Who was that?" My tone doesn't sound friendly.

"You smoke?" I look down and snuff it out, embarrassed that she saw me with it but ready to get back to the point.

"Who was that?" I repeat, trying to deflect. She looks at

the cigarette butt on the ground and takes a minute before answering.

"Uh, who? Inside?"

"Yes, Aveline." I want to scream at how jealous I sound, but I can't help myself around this girl.

"That was Pete. We went to school together—I've known him forever." She pauses. "What are you doing here?"

Relieved to hear that he's just a friend, I gesture toward her car. "I figured you drove this piece of junk and probably needed a safe way to get home."

Her smile disappears. "Well, you've wasted your time." She shoves past me and I reach out to grab her arm.

"Hey, seriously—it's not safe, let me drive you."

"I'm fine, Ethan. I don't need a ride."

I inhale, trying to calm the instant irritation I feel. "Please, Aveline." Her eyes study mine, and I would kill to know what is going on in her brain. *Geez, this woman makes me crazy.*

"Say you're sorry."

*What?*

"Sorry? For what?"

"For insulting my car." I realize maybe Aveline has an attachment to it and decide to let it be with a simple apology.

"Okay, I'm sorry. I didn't mean to offend you."

She smiles at me like she's won, and since I have no idea what we were fighting about, I just lead her over to my truck.

Once we're in, it's like everything goes back to peace between us. I look over and see her smirking then smile back at her. "What's with the grin?"

"I can't believe you picked me up."

"I didn't wanna have to haul you off the side of the road again," I tease.

She gasps and then sees me smiling at her. "You jerk!" She nudges my shoulder and we're right back to where we left off last night.

It may be late, I may have to be up at the ass crack of dawn, and I may be moving someday, but I wouldn't want to be anywhere else right now.

⸻

A few days later, I wake with a cold sweat covering my entire body, the nightmare leaving me trembling.

There's something about me that many people have learned over the years: ever since my parents died, I've been rather detached. I've never had a best friend. I've had girlfriends, if you can really call them that. Marie called herself my girlfriend, but I've never called any girl that since I was fifteen.

I don't like having attachments, though it's not because I'm an asshole, which I am. It's because I can't stand the thought of losing someone I care about again.

My dream was great at first. Everything was covered in greenery and it looked like Switzerland with lush trees and rolling hills of grass. It was beautiful. What's more was Aveline was there too, dressed in a royal blue dress and smiling at me while the sun shined down on her, making her glow like she was an angel sent down from heaven just for me.

I reach out for her hand and she reaches back. Just as our fingers are about to touch, she's pulled back. The scene changes and we're not in Switzerland anymore but in Ireland at the Cliffs of Moher. She's not watching where she's going, backing toward the edge like she has no control over what's happening to her body.

Her eyes are wide with fear and she scrambles against the force.

I'm running, sprinting, but I go nowhere. I can't reach her. I'm an inch from her when she falls, her screams piercing my ears. I scream her name and try following her over the edge, but suddenly the dream goes black.

That's when I wake up.

I'm grateful I don't have this dream often, but it haunts me while I'm feeding the cows and checking their water tanks to make sure they're not frozen. It's still imprinted in my brain when I'm showering off the morning, eating breakfast, and chugging my coffee.

It's still on my mind when I get into my truck and go to the one place I know I'll find relief. I pull up to her mother's bakery and get out. Before opening the front door, I take a deep breath to calm my thoughts and contemplate if this is where I should be.

I must be crazy to be here right now, but all I can think about is seeing Aveline, seeing her safe.

Pulling the door open, I'm accosted by the smell of cinnamon and fresh baked goods. This must be a tortuous place to work.

The younger girl who was here the first time I came in is behind the counter, and her eyes light up when she sees me. She holds up a finger then presumably runs to the back to find Aveline, and I'm grateful I don't have to ask.

I wander back to look at the pictures on the wall. They're photographs of Aveline and her mom, maybe five or so years ago. I remember that young Aveline. There are also pictures of her with her grandparents, her brother, and an older man who looks just like her brother; I'm assuming he was her father.

I'm looking at a picture of Aveline's mom with a man I assume was her husband, when a throat clears behind me. I spin to see Aveline, and just the sight of her makes me breathe a sigh of relief. I walk over to her before I think too much about it and crush her in a hug; she's caught off guard and stumbles into me. I catch her and just hold her for a minute. When I pull back and see her eyes, I know I need some time alone with her.

"You got a place we can talk for a minute?"

She nods and pulls me into the back of the bakery, but instead of taking me to the kitchen, she guides me all the way through the back door that leads to the small alley behind the building where I see her trusty Jeep parked by a dumpster. Opting to not make a joke, I turn and press her into the brick wall.

Aveline gasps a little in surprise as she looks into my eyes, and I seize the opportunity to take her lips with my own. I didn't come here to make out with her, but feeling her against me makes me want to come undone. I can't stop these feelings I have for her, and the intensity of them means one of two things: *fight or flight*. I didn't survive the military by being a coward.

I'm going to fight for this girl, whatever I have to do.

"Ethan?" Her shy voice breaks through my inner dialogue, and I pull away enough so we can both breathe. "Are you okay?" She rests her hands on my chest and I hold them with one hand, the other pressed into the wall by her head.

"Yeah." I release a breathy laugh. "Just wanted to see

ya." I'm trying to keep this conversation light since we've technically only had one date.

*Shit, is that really all it's been?*

"All right." She smiles but seems hesitant. "Are you sure you're okay?"

I change the subject. "Come over tonight." I don't ask.

She stares for a minute before nodding. "Okay. You gonna cook for me?" she ask playfully, and I nod my head.

"Of course—you'll need the nutrients." Her eyes widen at my suggestion, but she doesn't back down.

"I'll be there." With a smile, she leans up to kiss me again. I meet her halfway and we tangle for a few minutes before she has to go back to work.

I follow her back through the bakery to the front, where we see Lucas talking to the girl at the register.

"Come on, Katie," he teases, but she doesn't seem amused. When he sees us, his eyes light up in recognition. "Hey, guys." Katie whips her head back to us and looks to Aveline with crazy eyes. They probably mean something, but I have no clue what.

"Sup?" I say as I slap Lucas' hand. He seems like a cool enough kid, a little too happy for my taste, but at least he's not a punk-ass bitch like I was.

"Oh, just trying to get this one to agree to a date." He jerks his thumb over his shoulder, no concern whatsoever about her glaring daggers into the back of his head.

"You're a high school boy, Larry."

I quirk an eyebrow at him. "She hates that I call her Katie, so she calls me by the wrong name in retaliation," he explains.

I turn to Aveline, who seems to be paying no attention to the conversation, and she shrugs when she catches my eye.

"That's not your name?" I ask, reaching a hand out to shake hers and properly introduce myself. "I'm Ethan."

"Oh, I know." She gives me a look and glances at Aveline, who is bright red. "I'm Kate."

"Which is short for Katherine, which is long for Katie, which is long for Kate. I don't see the problem," Lucas says matter-of-factly. "Also, you just graduated last year, and your 'high school boy' stuff isn't going to be valid in like two months!" She huffs and greets a customer who's just walked in, and Lucas shrugs at me. "Women."

I start to nod but notice Aveline staring at me. She looks freaked out, but I don't know why.

"You okay?"

"Yup, great. Got to get back to work!" she practically squeaks. Quickly—so quickly I can't react—she plants a kiss on my lips and rushes into the back.

I stand frozen for a second then turn back to Lucas. He just smiles like a smug little bastard and points between the direction Aveline went and me. "So, you and my sister, eh?" He adds a Minnesotan accent to his last word.

"See you later, Lucas." I slap his back and walk out of the bakery. I have a date to plan.

## CHAPTER TWELVE

*Aveline*

I AM GOING to puke, or faint, or…I don't know, but it isn't good, and it isn't sexy. I've been sitting in front of Ethan's house for the past twenty minutes, and I can't make myself move.

When he showed up at the bakery this morning, I was so happy to see him. I was also happy because I'd assumed it was because he couldn't wait to see me like I couldn't wait to see him, but what I saw on Ethan's face wasn't elation. It was relief, which wasn't what I was expecting, and I don't know why he was relieved to see me like I'd left or something.

Then, he asked me to come over, and I freaked. I think I hid it well enough so he didn't realize it, but usually when a dude asks a gal to 'come over', they do more than just eat food. I'm not a virgin, but it has been a while, and Ethan is no celibate guy—at least I don't think so.

So, I sit here in my Jeep, rubbing my hands up and down my now smooth thighs (you best believe I went home and shaved every inch of my body below the neck). I'm glowing, and I mean that literally because I accidentally used my Peach Glow & Shine body lotion which has little pieces of glitter in it—a fact that, in my haste, I forgot. As a result, I sparkle. My blue dress was a light contrast to the shiny spots, and I decided to just go with the flow.

Five more minutes go by, and just when I am going to open my door, Ethan opens the front door to the house. I realize he was probably staring out the window in the kitchen, waiting for me to come in. He is probably coming out to turn me around and send me home. In that case, I wait for him to come to me. Why get out of the car if he's just going to make me get back in?

He motions for me to roll down my window and as I crank it, a smirk appears on his lips. I look away and stare at his house. I swear he can read my mind, but there's no sense in making it easy for him.

"You okay, hon?" It's the first time he's used a term of endearment, and it sticks in my brain on repeat. *You okay, hon? Hon, hon, hon.*

"Oh...yeah." I'm still looking at the house.

"Are you going to come in or is that still undecided?" The amusement in his voice is very clear, and I finally turn to look at him.

I contemplate my answer, knowing it will sound childish if I admit what was on my mind.

"Oh, ya know, just checking emails." I turn dumbly to

look for my phone on the passenger seat, mentally smacking myself.

He *mmhmms*. "Well, when you're finished with that, maybe you'd like to come in?" He's still smirking at me.

Gathering my stupid nerves, I wrench the door open, nearly knocking Ethan on his ass, and hop out. My skirt doesn't follow me down so I scramble to pull it back into place before he gets a pre-dinner show. My cheeks flush when I catch his eye, but he doesn't say anything, just gestures for me to walk ahead of him into the house.

When I step inside, I'm assaulted by the smell of fresh garlic and rosemary. Without an invitation, I walk into the kitchen so see what he has cooking, and I spy a large pot of boiling water sitting next to a pan filled to the brim with red tomato sauce and meatballs.

"Wow, this is some dinner." I turn back toward Ethan; he's standing with his hands in his pockets, watching for my reaction. I smile to let him know I'm happy about it, and his cheeks turn the slightest shade of pink. It's maybe the cutest thing I've ever seen.

He walks behind me, lightly touching my lower back, and reaches into the pantry by the fridge to pull out a box of noodles. "I know it's not homemade, but I think it'll taste all right."

"I'm sure this will be fantastic. Can I help with anything?"

He snaps his fingers like he just remembered something and spins away to reach for something on the counter. His fingers wrap around the top of an open bottle of red wine then he opens the dishwasher and grabs two freshly cleaned glasses.

"Sorry, I had to buy these today and wanted to make

sure they were clean." He sets the bottle on the little table where we've already had three meals, and when I remember my chili incident, my face heats again. *Why can't I just be normal?*

"You mind filling these?" He hands me one wine glass after drying it with a washcloth and dries the next one. When he hands me the second one, I carefully set them both on the table and slowly pour wine in each while he starts the pasta in the pot.

While the pasta boils, I hand him his glass and we toast. He smiles at me and my heart pinches, loving being here with him. Psh, what the heck was I so nervous about? I look back to Ethan's face to see him assessing my outfit, and suddenly my dress feels far too short. I tug on the hem.

"I like your dress."

I blush. *Damn, I really need to get that shit on lockdown.* "Thank you."

"I'm really happy you're here."

"Really?" I ask uncertainly. We had our date, which was amazing, then he unexpectedly showed up at my school and drove me home, but we've only texted a few times since. Ethan isn't a very big texter, and I was beginning to think the feelings were one-sided.

"Yes, really." He wipes away imaginary wine on his lips and sighs a little. "I'm not good at this."

"This being…?" I implore.

"Dating."

*Oh.* "Oh. Well, that's okay. We'll take it slow." I shrug, trying to show him I'm totally cool and relaxed about the whole thing even though internally I'm screaming at the fact that he called it 'dating'.

It apparently takes next to nothing to excite me.

"Yeah." He shakes his head, contradicting what he just said. "Actually, I don't know if I can."

Frowning, I just wait for him, mostly because I have no idea what to say or what he's thinking.

"I..." He stops, searching for the right words. "I woke up this morning and, without even thinking about it, came to see you."

I smile. This is a good thing...*right?*

"That doesn't exactly scream 'casual'." He's right, but he's not the only one who feels that way. I've wanted to see him since he dropped me off at my house the other night.

"Yeah, I guess not." My lip finds its way into my mouth as I chew on it. He stirs the pot of pasta, and we stay quiet for a minute. "Well, maybe we just see how it goes?" I shrug, not sure what he'll think of my suggestion.

"Yeah?" He looks so hopeful I want to give him a hug and assure him, so I walk up to him as he puts the spoon beside the pot.

"Yeah. What do you think?" Ethan gazes down at me, a smile on his lips, and I mirror him. Instead of answering with words, he wraps an arm around my waist, hauling me closer, and presses his lips to mine. We stay like that for a minute, but I crave to be closer to him. I juggle my wine to my other hand, but when I move my right arm to go around his waist, my hand catches on something hot, and I scream.

"Well, we have another fun story for the grandchildren," Ethan jokes, but I have a hard time finding any of this funny.

Turns out, I'm a fucking klutz.

Not only did I spill my wine all over him and partly on me, I broke the wine glass and sloshed the boiling water all over the counters and on the floor. My hand got the brunt of the bad burns, though, as I practically held it against the side of the pot.

Holding back tears while I run cool water over my hand at the tap, I wonder how soon it will be before Ethan realizes I'll probably burn down his house someday.

He sees the tears in my eyes and grabs a bag of frozen vegetables out of the freezer, wrapping it with a towel. He retrieves a paper towel and turns the water off, the temporary relief I felt from the water instantly receding.

I grab for the frozen veggies and quickly apply it to the burns. I'm still in shock. I look to see the mess I've made in his kitchen: there's still water dripping off the counter and wine on the floor, but while I ran the water over my hand, Ethan picked up most of the glass shards.

"I broke your wine glass."

He gives me a look. "It's fine—it was maybe two bucks." He searches in the pantry and finds another roll of paper towels. Ripping a few off, he starts to clean the floor. "I've been thinking about something since I met you," he says. *Here it comes, the 'how can anyone possibly be as big of a mess as you are' speech.* I brace for impact. "I've been thinking about buying stock in paper towels." I give him a confused look, and he stares until I catch on then he continues. "Bounty, maybe."

The understanding dawns and it must show because he starts laughing. I can't help giggling along. "Ha ha, very funny. I get it, I'm a klutz, but I can't seem to help it around you." We laugh for a few more seconds before he stands, dumping the rest of the towels in the trash.

"Something I don't understand: you work in a bakery, so aren't you around hot ovens all the time?"

"I'm as delicate as a rose petal in the kitchen," I say jokingly. "I'm pretty sure I can place the blame fully on you at this point."

"On me? What'd I do?"

"Oh please, like you don't know." He quirks an eyebrow. "I highly doubt this is the first time a woman was distracted by all your sexiness."

He laughs outright and loses his breath for a minute. I'm momentarily flushed from having admitted that out loud then realize I can't possibly make a bigger fool of myself than I already have. I could say, *Hey, by the way, I'm already pregnant with another man's baby but I really think this could work* and I still don't think I'd surprise him.

When he catches his breath, he straightens up and checks on the dinner I nearly destroyed. "Well…" He coughs, still smiling. "I think dinner is done. Keep that ice on your hand and grab a seat at the table."

I don't even argue; it could only possibly make things worse. I sit and watch him dish up the pasta onto our plates. I can tell from here it's more than I can eat, but I don't say anything. He reaches out and grabs a red Solo cup out of his cupboard then seems to think about something before grabbing two. He pours the remnants of his glass in one and pours more wine into the other.

When we're seated at the table, we both dig into our food, though I have to go slow since my right hand is temporarily out of commission.

"How is it?" he asks after a few bites, and I nod my head

toward him since my mouth is currently full of noodles. Some have yet to be slurped, and I imagine I look like a horse shaking its head with hay hanging from its lips.

 I finally swallow and vow to not take that big of a bite again. "This is surprisingly good."

 "Thank you. I made the meatballs from scratch."

 I shoot a brow up, impressed. "Really? I thought you would have bought frozen stuff."

 "Ah, I got a few tricks up my sleeve."

# CHAPTER THIRTEEN

*Ethan*

I'VE NEVER MET a clumsier girl in my entire life. Scratch that—I've never met such a clumsy *person* in my life. Since we met, Aveline's had several incidents. Technically her car accident wasn't her fault, but who wears flip-flops in a blizzard?

I feel bad she burned herself and slightly amused that it happened as we were starting up a heavy make-out session. This girl is anything but boring, that's for sure.

It was supposed to be a romantic dinner that hopefully led to something more, but with her injured, I feel bad even mentioning anything like that, even though she wouldn't really need her hand.

*Still*, I'm not *that* big of an asshole.

After we finish dinner, during which I watch her struggle valiantly with her left hand, we head into the living room with newly filled wine cups to sit by the fireplace. We don't need the heat, but the ambiance is worth it.

"How's your hand?" I reach to pull the ice off and she allows it. It's red and looks angry, and there's a little blister starting to form; it makes me wince for her.

"It'll be okay."

"I should get you some Tylenol." I start to stand but she grabs my arm with her left hand and keeps me in place. We're sitting on the tiny loveseat, the only thing there is to sit on aside from the recliner. We're squished together, and I can't help but enjoy it. I look at her and her eyes are kind, her smile sweet. I stay put and wrap my right arm around her shoulders, pulling her closer.

"I'd rather just sit."

"That's fine with me." We talk about our lives for a while. When she asks about the military, I tell her about the countries I've been to and how many missions I've been on, obviously leaving out the accident I was involved in. It's not something I like to rehash.

Once I feel I've fulfilled my duty of talking about myself, I turn the conversation to her. I ask where she wants to visit when she talks about traveling abroad and her eyes light up, making her even more beautiful.

"I'd love to go to Paris. It's touristy, I know, but I've always dreamed of it. I've even thought how amazing it would be to have a bakery there." She pauses. "But I wouldn't want to leave here forever. I also want to visit Italy—I do love pasta." She pats her belly and laughs.

"I've heard Italy is amazing—the countryside part, anyway."

She lights up again. "Yes! That's what I want to do, like, rent a car or something and go to different vineyards and try all the wine I can handle. That's number two, and Paris is my top priority." She smiles at me then pauses. Something she's thinking about dims her once bright expression, and I want to bring her smile back. "Can I ask you something?" Aveline asks, looking up at me with curiosity all over her face.

"Sure."

She breathes deep and summons her courage. "Why were you so rude to me at first? What changed?"

I don't answer right away, because I don't really know what changed. When I saw her at the party the town held for me, something in me shifted. I always thought she was cute in high school, though it wasn't like I pined after her all these years. In all honesty, I forgot all about her.

Then I came back and here she is, all grown up and gorgeous. I thought about staying away from her but couldn't stand that thought. Even though we both know our time is limited, it doesn't seem like we care. I mean, we're both here, aren't we? Finally, I answer the most honest way I can.

"At first, I didn't want to have any attachments, but then I decided I didn't care." I look into her eyes. "I wanted to try."

Her eyes soften then, and she leans toward me. Our lips meet directly in between us and with no hot objects too nearby—I purposefully put myself between her and the fireplace—we can relax into each other.

I'm surprised when her tongue finds mine first but allow her to lead us in this dance. Kissing her is unlike kissing any other woman I've ever been with. It's electric. Every touch from her makes me want to drag her into my bedroom and rip this blue dress from her body. It's been a while since I've been with anyone, and I realize I should probably take this slow.

Reluctantly, I pull away. She sighs like I took away her oxygen and finally opens her eyes. They're full of what you would describe as lust, but since I'm no fucking poet, I think it looks like she wants me to strip her naked as badly as I want to do so.

I clear my throat. "So, where else do you want to travel?" I'm trying, trying so hard not to take this too far. I've never cared about that before, but Aveline isn't that type of girl.

"Um..." She nearly fans her face then stops herself. She reaches to the floor where the ice for her arm slid off and replaces it. "Well, I've always thought Ireland would be amazing, you know. You see the Cliffs of Moher in movies all the time, and I think it'd be amazing to see in person." She smiles at me, and she doesn't know what she just did.

I can't stop myself—I stand as quickly as I can and grab her uninjured arm, walking her toward my room. We step inside and I turn the dimmer on low. My room was a mess this morning, but after we decided she was coming over, I made sure it was spotless. The bed is made to perfection with a brand new comforter and sheets, and I even found a candle at the store to light.

After earlier events, I decide to forgo the lighting of the candle. I lead her to the bed and turn her around. She's already panting in anticipation.

"Aveline," I say in a breathless voice. I don't want to talk, but I don't want her to run away screaming either. "Are you okay?"

She nods her head and rests her hand lightly on my

chest. I'm careful to make sure I don't touch the area of her burn and place my hands on her hips. I slowly drag one up to her neck and cup the back, bringing her lips to mine.

We start out slow, the opposite of what I feel like doing. She reaches up to the buttons on my shirt and, starting at the top, unbuttons them one by one.

I don't think she knows what she's doing to me. When she reaches the last button, she slides the shirt off my shoulders, and my hands immediately rip my undershirt off.

She lets out a soft gasp and I can't wait anymore. "Are you comfortable?"

"Oh yeah." I smirk at her answer when she runs her hands over my chest. I'm in shape, a habit that stuck with me after the service and is benefiting me well in this moment. I reach up behind her and grasp the zipper of her dress then slowly pull it down.

The garment easily falls to the ground, revealing her plain black cotton bra and panties. I know some guys prefer lingerie and I wouldn't complain if she were covered in lace, but this look is fucking sexy. It's the girl next door come to life.

"You're gorgeous." She blushes and giggles as she reaches back up for my chest. Suddenly, she looks nauseous. I bend to catch her eye. "We don't have to do anything you don't want to." It burns to say those words, but do I mean them.

"No!" Her outburst doesn't surprise me, and as I smile, she laughs at herself. "I mean, sorry, no, I want to." She scrunches her eyebrows in an adorable way and shakes her head, still smiling. "I want to do this with you."

I nod my head, incapable of speaking. I unbutton my pants, they fall to the ground along with my black boxers, and I wait.

She gulps, eyeing me up and down and down and up again until she meets my eyes. She keeps her hands to herself but leans her head up and kisses me on the lips. I smile at her shyness and reach behind her, closing the gap and unhooking her bra, allowing it to fall. Her breasts are perfect, and I show them some attention before bending down to remove her panties.

The moment of truth has arrived, and for the first time, Aveline is silent. We're both standing in front of each other stark naked, and then it's like a string that held our emotions together snaps and we are on top of each other.

I quickly relocate us so we're on the bed, her under me, and we're touching each other anywhere we can reach. When she wraps her hand around me, I lose my breath. It's been so long since I've been with a woman, and foreplay isn't going to happen for long this time. I'm not worried, though—if I have any say, this will be a first of many for us.

Finding my nightstand, I reach in, retrieve a condom—something else that was on my list today—and quickly tear open the packet. It takes approximately 3.5 seconds to roll it on and then I'm hovering over her again. Looking into her eyes, all I see is excitement and trust. "Are you ready?" She answers by pulling my head down for a searing kiss, and I push myself slowly inside of her until she's completely full. Aveline lets out a breathy moan and I struggle for control.

I kiss her again as I start moving, and right then and there, I know I'm done for.

# CHAPTER FOURTEEN

*Aveline*

MY OBITUARY WILL read, "Death by orgasm with a smile on her face." I ain't even mad about it, though Grandma might have a thing or two to say. Ethan is everything I've read about in fantasy novels; the bonus is that this is real life. I don't even have the words to describe how amazing this is.

He's cradling my head while lovingly covering me with tender kisses, rocking into me, and as I feel him getting closer to his release, I grasp his forearms, holding tightly. I'm nearing another orgasm and right as the fireworks shoot behind my eyes, he releases with a loud groan.

We're panting. It's the most exertion I've had in years, as embarrassing as that may be. Ethan collapses on top of me and rolls to my left side. He grabs my hand and kisses it. "That was amazing."

"Uh huh." Still out of breath, we lie there to gather ourselves, and when I turn to look at him, we both let out gentle laughs.

"Wow." He sighs a happy sigh and pulls my hand up to his chest.

"Yeah, sorry, it's been a while for me."

He crinkles an eyebrow. "You were amazing, but yeah, me too." He gestures to his leg, and that's when I notice a large scar.

"Oh wow." I lightly touch it with my burnt hand. "You haven't been with anyone since your accident?" Of course, I assumed something happened during his time in the military, but I haven't yet extracted the story from him.

"Nah, but I'm happy about that now." He smiles and leans up to kiss me on the lips then hops off the bed. He walks around the end, his limp a little more noticeable now, and guilt niggles at me. He goes out the door and down the hall to the bathroom to clean up.

I just lie there waiting for him, not the least bit ashamed of my nakedness. I think about what we just did and smile. I can't believe I slept with Ethan, can't believe he wanted to sleep with me.

I also can't believe I burned my hand! I raise it quickly to look at the angry marks on my skin. In my bliss, I didn't even think about the pain, but now that we're finished, it burns a little more fiercely.

"Here." Ethan returns with water and his hand held out. I extend mine and he dumps some Tylenol into my palm before handing me the water.

I sit up to take the pills. "Thanks."

"I guess I was in a bit of a rush to get in here and forgot about that." He chuckles and rejoins me in bed then untucks the blankets, and I crawl under them too.

It's a blissful moment, lying there with Ethan, no worries in the world in our post-sex haze.

---

I wake to the smell of bacon and coffee. I may just be in heaven right now; my body aches in the best places, and I'm hoping Ethan can handle another round before I leave.

It takes me a couple of minutes to wake up, and when I do, I realize it's morning.

It's morning—as in, the next day...as in, I stayed the *night*. I jump out of bed and bang my right hand on the nightstand in the process.

"Ah, fuck!" I cradle my hand for a minute and look down: of course, I never got dressed again, and I'm butt naked. I scan the room until I see Ethan's button-up lying on the floor; I snatch it up and throw it on. Yes, my dress is right there, but I'm a girl and who cares, right?

I rush out to the living room, searching for my phone. *Did I even bring it inside?*

"It's on the table," Ethan says from behind me, making me jump. I grab my chest and turn, and he gestures with the spatula in his hand while grinning at me. I take a moment to appreciate the naked chest he presents to me, wearing nothing but boxers.

"Oh."

"I answered a text from your mom..." He trails off as my eyes widen, wondering what she could have possibly said to me last night or this morning. I snatch the phone off the table.

**Mom:** I'm going to assume you aren't dead in a ditch somewhere and are at Ethan's. If that's the case, don't answer this.

I groan. Now my entire family knows I had sex last night. *Great.* She sent three more.

**Mom:** I know you're an adult, and I'm practicing for when you are in Europe by pretending you are in a different time zone and that's why you're not answering.

**Mom:** It's not working. Are you okay?

**Mom:** Ethan must be some guy.

She adds a winky face to that last one and I groan again. There's one more text, this one from me to her.

**Me:** I'm fine, Mom, sorry, my phone died.

"That's a lot of commas for one text." I grin at Ethan. "Do we have the same phone?"

"Uh, no idea."

"Well, apparently we do, otherwise I wouldn't have been able to answer her."

He thinks for a minute and looks at me again. "Gotcha." Turning back to the stove to continue working on breakfast, Ethan starts flipping the bacon.

I walk up behind him but don't touch—learned that lesson last night.

Then he says the words I yearn to hear every day: "There's fresh coffee."

I smile at his back. "Huh, someone's trying to get lucky again."

He doesn't even hesitate. "Hell yes." I giggle at his answer and revel in the comfort we feel around each other as he turns to look at me, eyeing my legs. "I like your shirt."

Laughing, I say, "Thanks, it's new."

After prepping my coffee the way I like it, I hurry out of his way. The kitchen is tiny, with barely enough room for one, and I don't want to get in the way of the preparation of my breakfast.

He sets down a stack of pancakes in the middle of the table and my mouth waters, but I resist. The table is nearly full after he's done setting it all down, and my eyes take in everything he's made.

"Hungry this morning, huh?" I tease. He grins back at me as he starts loading his plate, and I follow his lead.

"I worked up quite an appetite last night." He winks at me and my ovaries swoon. He's right; after we took a cat nap, he woke me again for another round, and this time, it was slow and sensual with him whispering in my ear how happy he was that I was there.

It was diary worthy.

We eat in comfortable silence. "How's your hand?" he asks, pointing to it with his fork.

I raise it and remember slamming it against the nightstand this morning. I decide to leave that out and tell him it feels better today.

"I was wondering, do you have plans today?" he asks while looking at his food, and I can't tell what he's leading up to. Does he want to ravage me in his bed all day long, not quite done with me? "I was thinking we could go for a drive or something, maybe into town, see a movie or whatever." He's clearly uncomfortable asking me.

"Sounds fun!" So does sex, but I keep that to myself. There's plenty of time for that later—*I hope.*

We drive to one of the bigger cities, about 45 minutes from Acton. I don't go into town often, so it's a treat, although being with Ethan is a treat in and of itself. The scenery is gorgeous, and we ride along listening to classic country music on the radio.

It's peaceful and the worries of my world (which are few) float away. All that matters is our time here together.

We go to one of the malls that houses the movie theater, wait in line, and pick some comedy that's playing. I couldn't care less what we see; it's just nice to be with each other.

We hold hands the whole movie, which in turn makes it impossible to focus, and I have no clue what the movie was about at the end. We walk around the mall window shopping, not taking anything seriously.

As it turns out, Ethan is actually pretty funny when he lets go of the tough guy persona.

It's a pretty perfect day. I never imagined being able to spend time with someone like this with no pressure. Ethan makes me feel safe, and yes, I am usually a mess in front of him, but he never cares. It's so new to me.

The trip I've been planning since high school is something I still looked forward to, though now I'm not so sure I want to go alone, which scares the crap out of me.

It's late in the day, almost dusk, and we are driving back to his place. I am dreading going home. It isn't that I couldn't stay, but I am terrified of getting too close too fast. Also, I need some space to figure out what the hell I'm doing.

Pulling up to the house, we both hop out. The cows are due for a feeding and Ethan has to get to work, meaning it's time I left.

"I had the best time," I tell him.

Ethan walks toward me and smiles a sweet grin before placing both of his hands on my cheeks and bringing my lips to his. It's a short kiss and when we pull away, he rests his forehead on mine. My eyes close, savoring this nice moment.

"I can't tell you how good this day was." It's the nicest thing he could've said. I peek my eyes open to see his gleaming back at me, and standing there in that moment, it is one I know to hold on to.

It's one I will remember for the rest of my life because it's the first time I've felt true love.

# CHAPTER FIFTEEN

*Aveline*

IT'S SNOWING AGAIN; that's how the spring months go in Colorado. Some days it will feel like summer is finally coming. All the girls unpack their dresses and the boys get out their shorts. We enjoy the sunshine, prep the gardens and the lawns, and start daydreaming about days spent on the lake, barbequing, and drinking around a bonfire.

Then, other days—days like today—we grudgingly get out our sweaters and shove into them, wishing we'd spent more time outside when the day was nice and dreading the damn driveway that needed shoveling.

Today, though, snow is the perfect weather to match my mood. I can't believe myself and my stupid freaking feelings. I am so scared I've gotten myself attached, and

I booked it home that night after spending the day with Ethan. When I walked through the door, I avoided my entire family and quietly snuck up to my room. I thought maybe my feelings were a fluke and had myself completely convinced it was all just a fantasy until I got a text.

**Ethan:** Had a great time. Can't wait to see you again.

I didn't know what to say without looking like an idiot, so I never replied. I felt the regret churn in my stomach, knowing he was probably waiting for some reciprocation. Thinking about my life was probably not what my mind should have done, but I couldn't help but wish I'd already left for my trip, knowing I never would have connected with him again and I could've avoided all the hurt I was definitely going to feel.

So, I did what anyone in my situation would do: I ignored the entire thing, 'forgot' my phone everywhere I went, and never answered any texts or calls. It's been four days now. I went to school once and was half expecting him to show up to pick me up again, but he never did.

I pinch myself for being an idiot *again*.

I am staring out the window in the back of the bakery, watching the snow fall heavily onto my Jeep and the alley; even that looks pretty covered in snow. I'm stirring my coffee with a spoon, thinking how it's really the only thing that has kept me from being a zombie the last few days.

"Ave." I jerk slightly at Kate's voice, sloshing hot coffee onto my hand. I hiss at the burn, grateful it isn't the hand still healing from the whole spaghetti incident.

Yeah, my mom laughed her ass off at that story. Of course, I left out the whole *I couldn't resist his sexiness* part.

"What's up?" I ask, running cool water over my hand.

"Are you doing okay?" She looks at me with genuine

concern in her eyes, and I stare at her for a minute, trying to figure out an answer.

"I'm okay." It's true. It isn't that I'm not technically okay. I am in okay shape physically, maybe not mentally, but still...

"Okay, can you help me with something in the front?" She gestures over her shoulder, giving me a small smile.

"No problem." I grab a small pack of ice out of the freezer, slap it onto my hand, and start for the front. I am staring down at it, seriously contemplating switching to iced coffee when I run right into someone.

"Oh! I'm sor—" My apology cuts off when I look into those bright blue eyes. Ethan looks even better than I remember. Yes, I realize that's dramatic, but four days is a long time.

"What are you doing here?" I look around for Kate, but she isn't anywhere to be found. *That isn't suspicious or anything.*

"Can we talk, please?" His polite tone is contradicted by his aggressive hold on my arm as he pushes me back into the kitchen.

I look down at my hand and try to not make eye contact, which is a mistake because I realize how dirty the floor is. *Add that to my to-do list.*

"Look at me." His tone is firm but I resist, not ready to give in. My stubbornness isn't something I am overly fond of, but I am who I am. "Look at me, Aveline." Ethan's voice softens and he steps toward me.

I look and—*damn, big mistake.* He looks so sad, and I am immediately ashamed of myself for how I've handled things.

"What happened?" He sounds so upset that tears almost

spring to my eyes, but I keep those bastards down.

"I don't know what you mean." *Liar, liar, pants on fire.*

"Don't." His eyes alight at my lie. "Don't lie to me. We had the best date. It was the best night of my life, and I know you felt that too. What happened?" He leans into me so I can't look away, and then I crack.

"I don't know what we're doing! I'm leaving soon." Technically, I don't know when I'm leaving.

"So what? So am I!" He isn't yelling, but the volume of his voice grows as he says this.

I'd forgotten that part. He's right, we're both leaving; it isn't like I'd leave him behind. Still...

"Then, what are we doing?" I stop and think about what I want to say. I decide lying isn't working so I'll try another route—the truth. "Look, I'm not someone who hides her feelings. I couldn't talk to you because I was already feeling real feelings for you, and I don't want to leave town with a broken heart. You just said you're leaving too, so what the hell are we doing?" I expect him to be angry or frustrated, but instead he is smiling at me. "What's the smile for? I'm serious."

"I know." He reaches for my face and, in his favorite way, grabs both my cheeks and smashes his mouth down on mine. I respond quickly and go to wrap my arms around him, dropping the ice pack to the floor in the process.

When he pulls away, his infectious smile makes my cheeks turn up. "I know this is stupid, I know we have limited time, but hell..." He stops and gives me a serious look. "I have feelings, too. Maybe this is temporary, maybe not—all I know is, I don't want to not be with you because we don't know what the future holds. We're in the present, and I want to be in the present together."

My breath is lost at those words, and instead of responding with something that might ruin the moment, I kiss him. A few minutes in, a throat clears. I didn't hear the back door open, but my mom is standing there, a canvas bag over her shoulder, arms crossed, giving us a knowing grin.

"Having fun, kids?" My cheeks burn red and Ethan gives a nervous laugh as my mother cackles in a way only mothers can. "I knew you had a better time than you let on, Aveline." She walks through the kitchen, completely pleased with herself.

"Hello, Mrs. Montgomery," Ethan says after he finds his voice.

It's funny that Mom can scare an adult ex-Marine. Waving her hand at him, she continues into the front of the bakery, letting us compose ourselves in private.

"Well, that was fun," Ethan says as he bends over to pick up the ice pack I dropped. I completely forgot about it. "What did you do now?" he asks, handing it over to me.

"Spilled coffee," I mumble, looking at my red hand, thankful it's not nearly as bad as the spaghetti burns.

Ethan takes my hand and kisses the red spot gently then takes the other hand, kissing that one too. He looks me in the eyes and his happiness is plain to see. "You need someone to watch over you." He says it nonchalantly, but I can't help but wonder if he'd be willing to take the job. I almost ask him if he has a passport but then catch myself.

I can't go from ignoring him to inviting him on an open-ended foreign vacation.

"Probably a bodyguard would do," I say with a smile on my face. It's easy to be with him, and I try my best to let go of the worries in my chest. What can it hurt to be with him, even if only for a while?

"Well, that could be arranged." He smirks and steps away, giving me space to move around the room. "We're having dinner tonight."

"I can't." I see him about to snap at me and quickly add, "I've got class."

Realization fills his eyes and he nods. "I'm picking you up."

"But then I have to leave my car."

"I'll take you to get it in the morning."

I crinkle my eyebrows. "But that doesn't make sense. Why take me home then pick me up the—oh!" I finally catch on to what he's trying to say, and he laughs at me.

"Yeah, that." He grabs me, holding me in a bear hug, and then he pulls back to look into my eyes. "Is that okay?"

I pretend to think about it, tapping my chin. "I think we can work something out." I finish with a shrug.

"You're a smartass when you're not trying to maim yourself."

He's joking, but I can't help responding, "It's not intentional!"

When he's done making fun of me, we manage to make it out to the front of the store where Kate is listening intently to whatever my mom is saying. They both look up at us when we enter, giant grins on their faces.

"Hey, you two," Kate says, wiggling her eyebrows. I roll my eyes and wish she were close enough to punch in the lady area. She's relentless.

"I've gotta go, I'll see you tonight," Ethan says before looking at my mom. "Goodbye, Mrs. Montgomery."

"Oh, Ethan! Before you go, would you like to have dinner at our house tomorrow?"

"What?!" I screech before I can help myself right as Ethan says, "That would be nice."

He looks at me with confusion and I try for a neutral expression. "If that's okay with you?" he asks.

"Oh! Yeah! Psh, of course!" *Foot, you remember mouth, right?*

"Okay." He leans in to kiss my cheek.

When he leaves, the two hounds pounce on me, and almost an entire hour passes before I'm able to get back to work. I leave my mom hanging with, "Oh, by the way, I won't be home tonight."

She gives me the mom look and I sprint into the back before she can leave her mark. *When did my mother get so scary?*

## CHAPTER SIXTEEN

*Ethan*

AVELINE TRIED HER best to ignore me, and part of me thought maybe that was for the best. She isn't wrong: we both have plans that will lead us to two opposite sides of the world and mean we'll eventually have to say goodbye.

My life is more complicated than it needs to be. I am struggling to get the farm ready to sell and have yet to put up the 'for sale' sign. I sent out some resumes for any leads on jobs in California, because I am going to have to get a job eventually—VA money for my leg is helpful, but not enough to sustain a regular lifestyle. It is all stuff that needs to be done, but all of it always feels like something I can do later.

I'm fooling myself: I'm pushing it off so I can spend

more time with Aveline, it's true. I'm not ready to say goodbye; we've only dated a couple of weeks, and I want more.

Driving to campus makes me happy because I know that less than twenty minutes from now, I'll be seeing her gorgeous face. I've wondered why she isn't already taken—she is the total package when it comes to a dream girl.

I am leaning against the passenger door to the truck—sans cigarette this time—when I catch sight of her leaving her class. She is smiling to herself, and I imagine she's anticipating seeing me as much as I am her. That guy from before runs up behind her again. *Man, he is relentless.* Doesn't he know she's taken?

They are chatting, and it looks friendly enough until he literally pulls her into a hug. I push myself off the side of the truck, ready to knock some sense into this asshole, but Aveline pushes against him, extracting herself from his hold. She says something to him, lightly gesturing with her hands.

I exhale a breath when she walks out the door but I don't wait. I walk right up to her and pull her to me, claiming her with my lips. Someone clears his throat, but I don't break from her and she doesn't even seem to notice.

When we come up for air, her eyes are glassy like I put her in a daze, and I grin. This girl has no idea that some prick is trying to get her attention, and I can't help but feel like a cocky bastard for being able to do that to her.

"Um, A-Aveline?" the guy stutters. He fucking stutters. *Pansy.*

She blinks at me and turns her head toward him where he awkwardly stands. Who stands and watches people make out?

"Oh, Pete. Sorry." She looks at her hands and realizes she is clutching my shirt. When she releases it, she shakes them out like she was holding on for dear life—maybe she was. "Um, this is Ethan, my…" She looks at me and is unsure about what to call me, so I fill in the blank for her.

"Boyfriend." I hold my hand out to him, even though I think he's a wuss. It doesn't help when he places his limp hand in mine. *Yeah, that's not a good sign.* "Nice to meet you." That's a lie if I ever told one.

"Oh." He doesn't reply with a normal response that humans should, like, I don't know, his fucking name. Then, as if he realizes what's happening, he stands to full height and looks at me with a glare in his eyes like I'm his competition. *Yeah right*—I've got inches on this guy in more ways than one.

"I'm Pete." *As in, Peter?* I want to ask but refrain because I don't want to embarrass Aveline.

"You ready, babe?" I wrap my arm around her shoulders and start to direct her away, not wanting to waste our time together with *Peter*.

"Oh, yeah. Bye, Pete!" She waves at him but doesn't look back. Instead, she leans into me and allows me to guide her to the truck. When she's in, I look back and see Pete is still standing in the same spot. I wave, he flips me off, and I laugh. I think it pisses him off because he stomps—yes, literally *stomps* off. This guy needs a life. What he's not gonna get is my girl. She's mine.

Aveline is lying on the bed, wearing only the sheet, and I can't believe the word pops into my head, but I can't help but think I love this girl. During my time in the military, I was never serious with anyone. I watched guys struggle to stay in relationships, and I never saw the joy in any of it.

But, had I been in contact with Aveline during those years, I'm not sure my stance would have remained the same.

I crawl back onto the bed after cleaning up and drag her over to me. She snuggles close and for the first time in years, I feel truly relaxed, content, and happy.

We stay silent for a while. When she turns her head to look at me, it's close to 1 AM, but neither of us are acting like we'll be sleeping any time soon.

"Ethan." Damn, even the way she says mine name gets me going. "Can I ask you something personal?"

"Of course." I stroke my hand through her long hair, watching it fall.

"Can you tell me what happened to you?" Her eyes glisten, and I can tell she had to work up the courage to ask me that question.

It's quite possibly the last thing on Earth I want to retell. I've done it so many times and I know when I'm done, I'll be exhausted. It's not just hard to tell the story about me; it's the fact of the tragedy that happened that day.

"It's not a nice story."

She cuddles closer and whispers, "You don't have to tell me, I just want to know you."

I sigh. I know she isn't giving me a guilt trip, but I can't help but feel like it's something separating us, so, I tell her.

"We were on a mission, a pretty routine one—we were sent out on patrols like this all the time. I was supposed to be riding passenger, but I had been up all night and my head was killing me so a buddy of mine, Brad, took the front seat. We were traveling along this long dirt road when we suddenly heard on the radio to turn back. We didn't turn fast enough and ran over an IED."

The scene unfolds before me like I'm still there and I feel myself sweating just telling the story, but I continue.

"It was a blur. It hit the passenger side, and I was on the same side, but it was under the front of the car. Brad died on impact, and I was injured badly. Most of the scars are from burns. Our other guys extracted us quickly but..." I take a deep breath. "The damage was already done. I was honorably discharged for my injuries, but I wanted to stay in."

She's quiet, and I wonder if she's asleep. Then she turns her head toward me, and there are silent tears streaming down her face. "I'm so sorry."

I hold her closer, trying to give her some comfort as I finish my story. "The worst part was David. He was Brad's best friend, and after what happened, he wouldn't speak to me again. He hates me for being the one who lived."

She gasps and shakes her head. "Why would anyone blame you? It wasn't your fault." She says it with such passion that I smile a little at her protectiveness.

"It's okay, I understand. His best friend died, and he hasn't been the same since. I've sent him emails and never got a response, but I don't blame him."

We lie in the silence, both of us mulling over what was just revealed. I know she's not going to hate me or anything, but that was my last secret and it's unnerving having everything about yourself exposed.

"I'm glad you're here." She sighs. "Not just alive, and I wouldn't have wished for your friend's death, but I'm glad you got discharged because otherwise you wouldn't be here with me."

"Can I ask one more question?" Aveline's voice is quiet and I lean down so I can look her in the eye, raising an eyebrow so she'll continue. "Why do you smoke?"

I smirk, not understanding why this needs to be asked but answer her anyway. "Well, it was a good stress-reliever in the Marine's, I guess old habits die hard."

Aveline looks down like she doesn't know what to say, but I feel like I know what she wants to say without her having to voice it. "Do you want me to stop?"

Her eyes find mine and the hope in them makes the decision for me. "Would you really?"

"For you? Anything." She smiles and my world feels light again and I can't help but kiss her. I know one thing is a fact, and it's that this girl—she's it.

I just don't know how to make that happen.

***

It's Friday and I wake without Aveline in my arms. I look around the room to confirm she's not there and then a smell hits my nose. I stand, throw my boxers on, and follow the scent to the kitchen. Aveline has some music playing in the background, a country song, and she's dancing around. The only thing she's wearing is my shirt as she pulls something out of the oven.

When she walks over to throw the oven mitt on the counter, I sneak up behind her and grab her around the waist. She squeals and turns.

"You ass!" She laughs and smacks my shoulder as I smile and kiss her on the mouth.

"This is the best way to wake up."

"What? Breakfast?"

"Nah, the show." I grin at her and she blushes, looking down at her outfit. She can't hide the smile on her own face, though.

"I'm sorry. I like your shirts."

"I'm not even a little bit mad."

We stand there until she directs me to the table. She pours me coffee, and I smile at how comfortable she is in my house. It feels right.

The smell turns out to be fresh banana muffins. They taste amazing and I say so as I shove half of one in my mouth.

"I don't know how you don't kill yourself at the bakery though." I laugh thinking about all the incidents she's had so far.

"I've had lots of practice, and besides, my 'incidents'"—she mimes quotation marks with her fingers—"are 100% your fault." She raises an eyebrow at me.

"My fault? How is that?"

"You distract me."

"I've never tried to distract you."

"It's all that sexy broodiness of yours. It's very distracting."

"Sexy broodiness, huh?"

She shrugs her shoulders. "Uh huh."

"I'll show you sexy broodiness."

"Oh, I bet you will." With those words, she's thrown over my shoulder, and she lets out a gleeful scream as we head back to bed.

# CHAPTER SEVENTEEN

*Aveline*

DINNER WITH MY mom, Lucas, and my grandparents was the last thing I wanted to do after spending my morning with Ethan. I've never felt as comfortable in my own skin as I do with him, and it was probably the best night we've had so far.

He finally opened up about his accident, something he hasn't wanted to talk about before, and it made me feel like I know him even better. I feel like I am important to him now.

Ethan, on the other hand, didn't seem to mind coming to dinner with my family; in fact, he seemed excited. "I want to know the people who raised you." Swoon, am I right?

He was the one having to talk me into it, and I knew

that deep down he was missing his own family and that was what was prompting his excitement. With that thought in mind, I did my best to put a smile on my face and brace for the embarrassing stories I was sure would be told tonight.

My mom, grandma, and I are finishing the last of the dinner prep when the doorbell rings and Stud immediately starts his incessant barking.

"Knock it off, Stud," I hear Grandpa scold. The door opens and I start for the front, but Mom hands me a bowl of salad with a sly look, pointing to the dining room. I sigh and finish helping set the table, allowing my grandpa time to grill Ethan.

Really, Grandpa is the least of my worries; it's Grandma I'm worried about. She's been quiet this whole time, and I just know she's compiling a list of things to ask him. *I'm not scared—you're scared.*

Finally, Ethan enters the dining room just as I finish arranging the food. I take him in: he's wearing dark blue jeans with a green button-up, and on his feet are nice dress boots I'm surprised he even owns.

He walks toward me and pulls me into his arms, not the least bit concerned with the eyes on us as he gives me a chaste kiss on the lips. I pull away first, reluctantly, and on the tip of my tongue are the words, *Let's get out of here*, but I manage to hold them back.

"Do you want something to drink?" I ask, licking my lips.

He smirks at me. "Sure."

I turn to walk into the kitchen, and whether it was him or me, I don't know for sure, but Lucas and I run right into each other. Not a big deal, except the sweet tea in his hand is now covering my entire dress, all over the front of my chest and down to my legs.

I gasp at the cold and glare at him. "Lucas!"

"What? You gotta admit we're both at fault for that one." He laughs, and when I look over my shoulder, everyone seems to be holding in a laugh as well.

"Oh, don't bother, just laugh it up." I wave my hand and march right upstairs, prepared to change my entire outfit. *Don't worry, I didn't spend the whole afternoon picking this out or anything. Oh wait...*

I rummage through my closet, noticing that everything is dirty, and I huff out a breath of air. I settle on a pair of mostly clean jeans and a nice shirt that has a barely visible stain on the bottom from where I spilled coffee. *Whatever.* I throw it on anyway. Hopefully, Ethan won't bother caring about what I'm wearing. At least Lucas didn't spill the tea on my head.

When I reenter the dining room, everyone is seated. The tea that was previously on the floor has been cleaned up and, bare feet and all, I walk around to my seat next to Ethan. He stands and holds out my chair, and I smile at him as I express my thanks.

Everyone is silent when I take my seat, and it's making me nervous. "What?" The second the word leaves my mouth, everyone starts laughing. I throw my hands up. "Okay, okay, the fun is over. Can we eat please?"

After that, everyone falls into easy conversation. We eat and talk about missing Old Carl. I don't say the first part of his nickname out loud anymore, but sometimes I can't help it in my head. That turns into talking about the ranch and what Ethan plans to do after he sells.

"Well, the plan is to head back to California." He avoids my eyes. I know that's his plan, but hearing him confirm it still hurts. "But I don't have any leads on work, so for now, I'll stay at the ranch and just take it day by day." He reaches under the table to place his hand on my knee. It's meant to reassure me, and it does the trick for now.

Mom takes the initiative and starts talking about the summer plans the town has. It's as small town as you can get when it comes to carnivals and festivals, and there's a farmers market every weekend that my grandma participates in.

"Are you planning on staying through the summer, Ethan?" Grandma asks. It's the first question she's asked, and it freaks me out that she's been so quiet.

"I think so," he replies with a smile.

"Well, might as well since Aveline doesn't leave until August." She says it so casually then takes a bite of the pie we've moved on to. He didn't know I was planning on leaving in August, and I think her words catch him off guard.

He looks at me and asks, "You leave in August?"

"Well, yeah, if I can finish my classes by then," I say quietly. He nods, and I can tell he doesn't want to talk about it here.

"Which you will. You've worked hard for this opportunity, and you'll finish in plenty of time," Grandma says sternly, and I nod at her. She's right—I've worked my ass off for this trip, trying to finish college and working whenever I could. I just never expected to get sidetracked by a guy. I look at Ethan to gauge his reaction.

"Well, then we'll have a hell of a summer." He smiles, and I'm so relieved I release a breath I didn't realize I was holding.

We talk about random stuff during the rest of the meal, including Lucas' plans after graduation. When questioned, he answers, "Eh, it's up in the air." He's so easygoing, but that kind of stuff was never important to Lucas, although I think his mind is more focused on *who* than *what* these days.

When we're finally finished with dinner, Grandpa takes Ethan out to the barn to "show him around", or, in other words, grill him. We send Grandma to relax with her book, and the three of us clean up.

"So?" I ask Mom and Lucas as we wash dishes.

"I like him," Lucas says. No surprise there—he likes everyone.

"I do too," Mom says hesitantly. "But, I do worry for you honey. You're both leaving." Her eyes show her worry.

"I know." I sigh. "But we tried not seeing each other and it didn't work for us."

"Ave, look, I'm not going to intervene because I'm not that kind of mama, but I will say this: I don't want you—either of you—to compromise your lives. Even if you part to go your separate ways, you can always come back together again." She pauses, and I don't say anything, mostly because I don't have anything to say. "You're both young. Just don't rush things."

I nod. I understand where she's coming from and I get it, but she doesn't know how I feel about him, doesn't know what he's been through.

On the other hand, she's right—I can't compromise. For the first time, maybe ever, I'm lost.

Waiting on the front porch swing for Ethan and

Grandpa to come back, my mind wanders to the place I don't want it to go: the future. There's no denying I'm scared. I know what I want when it comes to my future, but I didn't anticipate Ethan coming into my life. Now, I'm not sure continuing to date him is the best thing to do.

*This can only end badly, right?* That's the last thought that pops into my head before Ethan comes around the corner with Grandpa right behind him, laughing at whatever he just said. It's a picture I never thought I would see, my grandpa connecting with a guy I'm dating, and that in itself has me questioning my doubts.

Ugh, why can't I just make up my mind?

"All right, well, I'll leave you kids to it." Grandpa shakes Ethan's hand and pats my shoulder as he walks into the house.

Ethan takes the seat next to me and grabs my hand as we rock back and forth. We don't say anything for a while, just enjoying the quiet that surrounds us.

"So," I say, breaking the peace, because that's what I do. "How was your night?"

Ethan turns his head to mine. "It was great."

I crinkle my eyes at him, not convinced. "Really?"

"Yeah, your family is great. I like them." He keeps pushing us back and forth, back and forth. My feet are no longer helping while I stare at him, sure he's going to crack and tell me they're crazy. "Why are you staring at me?"

"I'm just waiting for the punch line."

He chuckles and tucks me under his arm; I don't resist. "There isn't one. Really, your family is nice. Your grandpa has some good ideas to make my uncle's place better so it will sell faster."

"Oh." So, they talked real estate.

"Yeah, but I told him I was going to wait until at least July before I put it up."

"Why July?"

He looks into my eyes then and they soften. He's so relaxed right now, and it makes me wonder how I'll ever be able to leave him when the time comes. "Because I'm not leaving until you do."

Simultaneously, my heart melts and clenches. "Do you think we're being stupid?"

He sighs and looks away. "How many times are you going to ask me that?" I shrug and look away. "Let's just enjoy what time we have together. We don't have to make this a thing."

I don't answer because I'm afraid I've already let my pesky emotions get involved in making this the definition of 'a thing'. We stay like that, cuddled and content until it gets late. We decide it's best that I don't go over to his place. "Just this once," he says with a wink, and I immediately want to jump in his truck.

When I'm lying in bed, I push the negative thoughts away and imagine what our summer is going to look like. This will be the best summer as long as I can keep my emotions in check and go with the flow.

My phone buzzes and I look at it.

**Ethan:** I can't wait to spend my summer with you.

It's simple, but knowing he's thinking what I am right now makes me giddy to see what the next few months hold.

**Me:** Me either.

*Yeah, bring on the summer.*

# CHAPTER EIGHTEEN

*Ethan*

SUMMER HAS OFFICIALLY arrived, and you can smell it in the pine trees all around. Working on a farm in the summer is hot, sweaty, and sometimes nasty, but it's one hundred times better than the spring time. The spring is unpredictable weather and horrible mud. Some days you're breaking ice in the water troughs and others you're watching your cows struggle to stand because the rain made it so muddy they can't help but slip.

There are other things that are enjoyable in the summer too, and coming up to the house for a break, I see my new favorite thing about this season: *blue jean shorts*.

Aveline is here all the time, per my request. She's all but

moved in with me over the last few weeks, though we've avoided talking about anything too serious and are taking the whole go-with-the-flow thing seriously.

Right now, she's got a book perched in her lap while she basks in the sunshine. The sun has already made her hair lighter; it's a little longer than when we met, nearly reaching her ass, and I love it. The white tank top she's wearing reveals small amounts of sweat popping through, and I wish I had my camera so I could capture this sight forever.

She looks up when she finally hears me and smiles a beaming smile. God, I love making her smile. I've never spent so much time with a woman before. I dated Marie in high school, but I didn't come close to actually spending quality time with her like Aveline and I do.

Also, my feelings for Marie were nowhere near what I feel for Aveline. The girl is my light, and I'm terrified letting her go is going to send me back into the darkness.

When I approach, she sets down the book she's reading and I glance at the title: *A Guide Through Paris*. My heart clenches painfully but I shove it to the back of my mind. One day at a time.

"Hi, gorgeous." I smash my lips to hers and she responds immediately. I'm sweaty from working in the hot sun but she doesn't care, running her hands over my shoulders and into my hair.

"Hey there, you hungry?"

My stomach answers her and we chuckle. I hold the door open for her and when we walk inside, my nose smells bacon. I'm curious. "You made something?" The cooking has been my job from the start of our little fling, other than baked goods, of course.

"Well, not really—just BLTs." She sets sandwiches on

the table for us and grabs a pitcher of lemonade and glasses. I take my seat right beside her and gulp down the lemonade immediately. Once my thirst is taken care of, I dig into the sandwich with a loud moan.

Aveline smiles at me and digs into her own food.

That's how we are: we flirt, we hang out, we eat.

We completely enjoy being around each other. There have been a few nights where she goes home, just to keep things slightly casual. It doesn't actually work, but it makes her feel better so I let it go.

Her family has accepted me completely, and it's the best feeling. I forgot what it was like to have a real family. My parents were awesome and I treasure all the memories I have of them, but when I moved in with Uncle Carl, it changed everything. He wasn't a bad guy, he was just quiet and kind of made me that way too.

The day ends the same way it started—with Aveline in my arms—and again, I don't know how I'm going to let her go.

It's the annual summer kickoff carnival and the entire town is here, along with people from some surrounding towns. The main street of Acton has been totally transformed into a real carnival. The booths cover every inch of the road, and there are rides down at the end by the mill. There's face-painting, funnel cakes, lemonade stands—you name it, they've got it.

I've been to one of these in my life, and it wasn't enjoyable, if I remember correctly. This time, though, will be different, and I think I can thank the company for that. Aveline's sunshine attitude mixed with a carnival is something I can't wait to experience.

Pulling open the door of the bakery where I'm picking her up, I get hit by the delicious smell and bypass the front counter. Kate gives me a wave, and it reminds me of the first time I was in here, the day I officially met Aveline. It's amazing how much can happen in such a short time.

Aveline is frosting cupcakes. Her back is to me and she's wiggling her ass around as she works. There's soft country music playing through speakers on one of the shelves, and she sings along. All alone back here, she's in her element, and it's relaxing to watch her work, but I can't wait anymore.

"Whatcha doin?" I ask, purposefully trying to spook her. It works—she jumps and squirts frosting all over her fresh cupcakes. I cringe a little and chuckle behind her.

"You jerk! You did that on purpose." She huffs and tosses the frosting onto the counter. Turning, she crosses her arms and quirks an eyebrow.

"Oh hon, don't be mad at me. I was just messing with you." I walk over and wrap my arms around her, but she resists and doesn't let her arms down. I nudge her lips with mine, trying to get her to open up, and she finally relents. Her arms don't immediately go around me and I think she might shove me, but then I see it, just a second too late.

"That's what you get!" she yells, giddy laughter tumbling from her mouth. I can't really see her anymore due to the frosting attached to the cupcake that was just smashed all over my face. *That little...*

"Oh girl, you're in for it." Wiping the baked good off my face, I reach behind her and grab one of my own. Her eyes widen and she turns to run, but I grab her and find her face with the cupcake. We're both laughing, and I haven't ever felt so free, even with frosting all over us.

We finally stop struggling and she turns to me. We chuckle at the mess and start to clean up.

"Well, I may have messed up all of those, but it was worth it." She leans up to kiss me, and I reciprocate.

---

The carnival is definitely one like you dream about as a kid. Everything is lit up even though it's not totally dark yet, and Aveline is even more fun than I thought she'd be. She stopped to break a twenty so she could play the games and refuses to let me pay for everything.

I think we've literally played every game twice over—she's stubborn and likes to win, another thing I've learned about her. She's smiling the entire time, though, and it makes the event even more fun. She's scared of the Ferris wheel, which shocks me, knowing how adventurous she seems to be. I finally talk her into it and she oohs and aahs the whole time. I can't wipe the smile off my face for anything.

"This is amazing!" She laughs as we get stopped at the top, allowing someone to get on or off. The light in her eyes is the brightest I've ever seen, and I vow to keep it lit as much as I can.

"I can't believe you've never done this."

"Well, no one has ever cared enough to get me to try." She smiles in my direction. "I guess I needed the right partner."

I open my mouth to tell her I'll be her partner in anything she wants but stop myself. The last thing I want is to scare her off. I settle for replying, "I'm glad I could help."

After the Ferris wheel, we decide we're going to get the fattiest, most sugar-filled thing we can find. Aveline tells me she needs to run to the restroom and I watch her go, wondering how someone as fucked up as me could get so lucky.

Then I turn and my luck runs out.

# CHAPTER NINETEEN

*Aveline*

I'VE NEVER HAD a better time at one of Acton's carnivals. It's one of those things I secretly love but tried not to let on about before. Going with Ethan makes the experience fun and easy to get into, though. I've dragged him through every game more than once, and we've also done a couple of rides. He hasn't complained at all.

I tried going with Jared in high school, but he hated every second of it, and when he said we should go to the old mill, I ditched him for a book at home in bed. Definitely not feeling those feelings tonight.

I rush to the restroom, in a hurry to get back to Ethan to enjoy the rest of our night. *Damn small bladder! You curse me again.* Just kidding, but seriously, how do guys hold it for so long? It's a mystery I'll never understand.

I finish up and do that whole *flip your hair upside down* thing you see in movies, but instead of making it look nice, it poofs it up. Groaning, I try to smash it back down onto my head and then realize I've been standing here for at least five minutes. What a waste, and Ethan probably thinks I'm doing more than peeing. Shrugging at myself in the mirror, I leave the restroom in search of the hot Marine I get to call mine.

Smiling like an idiot, I look around, but I don't see him where I left him. I scan the area and see Marie, his ex who we ran into briefly on our first date. She's standing at one of the game booths with some guy. I ignore that until I look closer and see the guy she's with is Ethan. She has her hand running over his arm, and he's laughing at something she's saying.

I watch for a minute and they continue like they're having a great time. I wait for him to shove her hand off and when he doesn't, I feel my eyes heat. It pisses me off that I want to cry. We've said again and again this is just for the summer, so why do I feel so hurt?

Not wanting to wait around for the answer, I walk in the opposite direction, thankful I can disappear behind the bakery.

I don't leave like I thought I would. Instead, I open the back of my Jeep and sit on the edge, my feet swinging back and forth underneath me. I take a deep breath and love that I'm smelling the fresh summer air. Winter felt like it lasted forever, and I'm so glad summer is finally here.

It has me thinking about going to Paris—I've decided I want to start there. It's my most coveted place to visit, and in case I go through money too quickly, I don't want to regret not making it that far. Deep in thoughts of the trip, I don't notice the figure turning the corner in a hurry.

"Aveline!" Ethan looks out of breath and like he's going to pass out as he runs toward me. I'm expecting him to be pissed that I ditched him, but the look in his eyes is worry, not anger.

"Shit, where did you go? I've been looking for you for an hour!" He crushes me to his chest and it knocks the wind out of me. I slowly reach my arms out, thoroughly confused by the reaction.

"Sorry, I guess I didn't want to interrupt." I look at my feet, not wanting to admit how much it bothered me that he was flirting with her. *Dammit! I'm not supposed to care this much!*

"What the hell are you talking about?" He sounds confused, so I give in, though reluctantly.

"I saw you with Marie." I'm ashamed to say I sneer her name. *Sue me.* "You looked happy, so I thought maybe you wanted to catch up."

He lets out a laugh—well, it's more like a scoff, but he's smiling. "I was fake laughing at something stupid she said."

"She was touching you." *Shut up, shut up, shut up.*

"She wasn't. Plus, I kept looking at the bathroom door, hoping for an escape." He sits beside me in the Jeep and wraps his arm around my shoulders. My treacherous body gives in to him. "How'd you sneak past me?"

"I didn't even try—I stood in one spot for like five minutes." I stare at the ground, waiting for the crack in the asphalt to open up and swallow me whole.

"Ave." He grabs my face and turns it toward him so I have no choice but to look at him. "I don't want anyone else. You're it for me." My breath stalls until he finishes. "For the summer, I mean."

I think he blushes slightly, but he doesn't give me a chance to call him on it before his lips are on mine. His words ease my clenched heart a little, and we spend the rest of the night wrapped up in one another. I can't help but hope this summer feels as long as the winter does so our time together doesn't disappear too fast.

"Now, come on, we need a funnel cake." I stare at the hand he holds out to me, marveling at the man who has opened up to me these last few weeks. I smile, happy, and take his hand, ready to jump.

Laughter—that's what I remember when I'm lying in bed that night. It's late, maybe two in the morning, but I can't sleep. My cheeks hurt from the smile I can't get off my face; it's probably a permanent feature for me after tonight.

Ethan is funny, like really funny. After he helped me get over my jealous streak with Marie, we didn't let go of each other the entire night. I'm sure this will be the lead for the town gossip column tomorrow, but I couldn't care less. Hell, if they called right now, I'd give them an exclusive. *Are you happy?* Hell yes. *Is Ethan everything you wished for in a partner?* Um, I'm pretty sure Jesus himself crafted Ethan for me, so...yeah. *When will you start having babies?*

That's about where I'd cut off the interview. Okay, so maybe I wouldn't be into a full-out interview, but the happiness I'm feeling right now is more than ever before.

We went through almost every vendor at the carnival, all of whom I've known my whole life. They all felt the need to tell Ethan every embarrassing story about me they could remember, but he didn't seem to mind much. In fact, he would pull me closer every time he heard another one.

My brain is tired after the long day, but my imagination runs wild with possibilities. How hard would it be to wait to leave until next year? Ethan could stay longer, maybe find work here, and then we could truly know if we work.

It's a silly thought; that isn't even a question—we just work. We're like peanut butter and jelly, Johnny and June, Pinky and The Brain... Well, whatever, we work, and that is all that matters.

Because of that, I suddenly have no desire to leave home. I picture my life like I'm flipping through a homemade scrapbook, seeing pictures of me in the bakery, Ethan visiting me for lunch. I imagine having a meal ready for him when he gets off work. I imagine him proposing, a perfect princess cut diamond, nothing flashy but something to say, *She's mine.* The wedding is next, something small, family only up on a mountaintop, and then would come the babies. We'd have at least two.

It's a pretty picture I paint for myself, and not one of those things includes me traveling. Part of me thinks, *Who cares? I get the American dream,* but then there is sixteen-year-old me, the one who read travel books for fun, planned an entire European trip without a penny to her name, and has been saving money for years to be able to afford it.

The thoughts keep swirling around and around in my

head until I don't even know what the right answer is. A beeping sound interrupts my thoughts and I reach for my phone on my nightstand, immediately smiling when I see who's calling.

"Hello?" A sigh comes through the phone.

"So, you're up too, huh?" Just the rumble of his voice makes me want to curl into the memory of our laughter from earlier in the night.

"Yeah, can't sleep after such a busy day, I guess."

He chuckles. "It was a good day." He paused. "But tonight was even better."

My grin grows. "I have to agree."

"I wish you were here with me." He sighs again, and I hear him move around. I think about him in that bed and feel an urge to get into my car and see him right then and there.

"I do, too," I confess, not even remotely ashamed.

"Come over."

I pause and think about that. It's two AM. I don't work in the morning—thank God, because I would be useless. I think about how maybe being together too much might make things harder down the line.

"Ave, I want to see you."

Knowing he feels the same way I do makes my answer easy.

"Okay."

# CHAPTER TWENTY

*Ethan*

THIS IS WHAT *is meant to be.* That's the thought that sticks in my mind as Aveline cuddles closer to me. It's almost four in the morning and she finally fell asleep. We didn't waste any time when she walked through the door.

I paced by the front window, waiting for her to get here. As soon as she agreed, I was out of bed and watching. I didn't let myself think about it too hard, the need I felt to be by her. Instead, I just let it be. It was the happiest I've ever felt, and I wasn't about to ruin that with negative thoughts.

Her headlights shone through the window and I was out the door. She didn't get hers open before I was right there to grab her. I kissed her right away, not wanting to let her overthink being here, knowing she was probably freaking out about it the whole drive over.

She responded by melting into me and I dragged her into the house, straight to bed. We didn't speak, communicating with our bodies instead. Some say you need words to convey how you feel, but not us; we can have a whole conversation with our body language.

Having been together a few times, we knew each other's moves. She moved one way and it told me what she needed; I moved a certain way and she knew what to do, and tonight, we moved perfectly.

Something happened last night. A switch was flipped in me as we moved together, a powerful pull that told me no matter what, I can't let this girl go.

So now, staring at her lying in my arms, content and dreaming away, perfectly comfortable with me here—I know it isn't a fluke. This isn't some summer fling for us, not anymore. I don't know how I am going to convince her to give us a shot, but I know I have to do everything it takes, even if I have to wait for her.

It's a Saturday and early as fuck. I normally like getting up early so I can beat the sun to work every day. Last night Aveline was over late and we talked until nearly one in the morning, even though she had to be up early to help her grandma with the farmers market she participates in every weekend. Knowing she would get an ass chewing if she was late for that, she decided it was better to receive that in her own room than have her grandma show up at my place.

It was something I'd be fine with, but Aveline holds back on intertwining me with her family. I know it's a big step to be involved in the family stuff, but now that I am set on being her future, I insert myself wherever I can, which means going to the farmers market to help with the family business.

It's still early when I make it down to Main Street, but most of the town is already there, and I can't wait to see Aveline's face when she sees me. It takes a few minutes to find her booth with all their items displayed. They have jams her grandmother made, muffins and doughnuts Aveline and her mom usually sell at the bakery, and there is even handmade jewelry on the table, though I have no idea where that came from.

She is turned away from me when I go up to the side of the booth. Her grandma sees me and gives me a little smirk but doesn't say anything, just goes back to talking with a customer at the table. I am able to sneak around without Aveline noticing, and I reached for a place she can't stand to have touched, right on her sides.

"AH!" She whips her head around and smacks me in the head. It's not a hard hit, but you'd think she broke my nose with how she's acting, her hand covering her mouth as her eyes widen in surprise. "Oh, my gosh! Ethan!"

"Hey." I rub my head for emphasis and grin at her. "Mean right hook," I joke.

"I'm so sorry! I don't know why you'd do that—you know how clumsy I am." She reaches out to check the damages, and she's close enough to kiss so I do so discreetly before she can get away.

We pull back and smile at each other. She leans up and

hugs me, and it's so innocent and loving that I can't help but grip her back tighter.

"What are you even doing here?" She glances around me to her grandma, who shrugs.

"I didn't know he was coming, but since he's here, you two hold down the fort. I need some honey." She pats me on the shoulder, and I think I just got the seal of approval from her grandmother.

"To answer your question, I came to help out." My assumption that this might make her uncomfortable was wrong—she grins so big it's possible it could get stuck.

"Well, damn. That's pretty great." She gestures toward the table and gives me a rundown of all the goods. Jam is quite expensive, and when Aveline gets to the jewelry, which is individually marked, I ask her where they came from.

"I make them. I started in high school to sell here for extra money." She pauses, and her eyes turn sad. "For my trip."

Her trip, of course, is still set to begin at the end of summer. "Well, they're awesome," I praise. "Where do you find time for everything?"

"Whenever I can, usually nights, though not so much these days." She giggles, referring to our nights together. "But I had inventory stocked up, so I'm pretty well set for summer."

Just then a couple comes up to the table, and Aveline dives into conversation about the homemade jams. I mostly sit back and watch, noticing how personable she can be. She lights up when she talks about her family and the amazing products they offer.

The woman buys a necklace, and Aveline puts the

money in a separate container from the one the jam money went in. I realize it's her trip fund, and the amount of cash in there makes me realize how serious the trip is and how my time to make her see that we can't possibly end this after summer is dwindling.

We spend the better part of the morning selling off most of the jams and baked goods. She only sells a few pieces of jewelry, but she doesn't seem too concerned about it and keeps a smile on her face. I find every excuse to touch her. Reaching for a bag under the table, my hand brushes her bare leg; putting money in the box, hand goes to her waist "so I don't fall over." Any reason I can find, I use.

It's midday now and I can't believe this thing is still going on when a familiar face comes up to the booth.

*Pete.*

God, I hate this guy. He's clearly surprised to see me behind the table with Aveline but ignores me and strikes up a conversation with her.

"Hey, Ave, how are you doing?"

Aveline smiles politely. "I'm great! How are you? You weren't in class on Thursday."

He sighs, and I swear the dude should just be a chick. "Yeah, I was pretty under the weather—stomach virus."

Gross.

"Oh no! I hope you're feeling better." *Damn, she's too nice.* I relax into the camping chair I was resting my knee in. She's not into this guy, and as much as I doubt he could steal my girl, it's nice to see it for myself.

"Much. I actually came over to ask you something." I perk up. *Whatcha doin' Petey?*

"Oh?"

"Yeah, a bunch of us are having a little high school

reunion tonight, a bonfire for old times' sake, and I was wondering if you'd want to go." This guy can't be serious.

Aveline tenses, obviously feeling awkward to be put on the spot. I mean, the guy just asked out my girlfriend right in front of me. I stand then, making myself a part of the conversation.

"Hey man, sounds fun. We'll be there." Pete clearly wasn't expecting that at all. *Yeah, well, this ain't high school, boy.*

"Oh." He's disappointed, but I couldn't give a shit less. "All right, see ya." Not even looking at Aveline, he walks away. *Douche.*

Aveline turns to me with an eyebrow quirked. "You want to go to a bonfire?"

*Shit.* I didn't really think about that, but I don't want to make it a big deal. "Yeah, why not?"

"Because it's all the people I avoided for four years." She looks out into the road where everyone is filtering around, and I sigh with relief thinking she's going to say we don't have to go. "But it would be a little fun now that I have you."

*Shit, again.*

"Sounds like a good time, babe."

High school reunion, here we come.

# CHAPTER TWENTY-ONE

*Aveline*

BEING AT A bonfire is like walking back in time. It's only been three years since I walked hallways with these people, but it feels like it's been a lifetime. So much of my life has changed in just a short couple of months, and I feel like a different person.

I've been achieving my goals since I graduated high school. Even though I wanted to do all my traveling last year, at least I'm still going to do it. Dating Ethan is a whole other factor, and it's so weird to see that everyone here remembers him.

It also makes me feel like an idiot that I didn't remember who the guy was a couple of months ago and now not only are we together, this bonfire is like welcoming back the town hero. It's like the welcome home party but with people our age instead of all the parents.

"Hey, Ethan! Welcome back, buddy!"

"Ethan! We missed you!"

"Hey man, thanks for your service."

And so on and so on. It's insane, and I don't really think Ethan is a big fan of the attention. Every time someone comes near him, he tenses into me, and I squeeze his hand to reassure him. He smiles politely and thanks each person.

Soon enough, we have plastic cups and are sitting in front of the big bonfire. I've never wished so much for us to be alone—this might actually be romantic if that were the case. Instead, the women of the group sneer at me. "Oh em gee, that is not *Aveline Montgomery* with Ethan Sexy-Pants Hart."

No joke, I heard that line spoken from actual lips tonight, and not at all subtly.

I get it, I do. I'm the nerd of the school. I hung out with a handful of people, but not all the time like everyone else. I liked my books, I liked my music, and I liked my privacy, which is why I think I had no idea Ethan even existed.

*Ethan Sexy-Pants Hart.* The nickname made me snort, and he thought I was choking, patting me on the back.

"So." I lean into him, and he wraps his arm around my shoulders. "Seems you were quite popular in high school, eh?"

He grimaces like he doesn't want to comment; the silence stretches on and I don't think he's going to reply, but then he finally opens his mouth. "This is a small town, and I don't think the kids were used to someone like me."

"Someone like you?"

"Yeah, I guess you could say I was less than a good guy."

"Wait, wait, wait." I smirk at him. "Are you saying you were a bad boy?" I hold in the laugh I want to let out.

"I guess so." He takes a drink of his beer and studies the fire. "I wouldn't have been good for you back then, that's for sure."

"Hm, I don't know about that."

"Oh? You think you would've dated the bad boy?" His face transforms into playful Ethan.

"I think so—had I known you existed."

He shakes his head and exclaims, "I can't believe you didn't know me!"

"Whoa, careful, your cocky is showing." *Snort, giggle.*

"Okay, but I was the star of the football team. I had girls all over me, and guys wanted to be me. All I did was look for you every day, and you had no clue I was even someone you went to school with. How is that possible?"

I pause and absorb all the words he said, one thing sticking out above all else. "You looked for me every day?"

He blushes, and it's the first real blush I've ever seen on him. "Well, you were intriguing. I don't think I ever really saw your face, but I know it was you."

Thinking back, I never walked around school without my nose shoved in a book.

"I wanted to talk to you, to know you, but I wasn't any good in high school." He looks down at his beer swirling around in his cup and I take a sip of mine. "I think your mom called me reckless."

I do choke on my beer this time and try to discreetly wipe my nose. "What? My mom?" I turn on him fully now and eye him.

He looks sheepish. "Yeah, she may have caught me with a girl once."

"What? When?"

"Homecoming." I stop to think. I didn't go to any dances—it wasn't my thing at all—but that didn't stop MaeBelle Montgomery from attending the socials in Acton, even if she had to chaperone, which she did.

"Oh, yeah."

We fall silent then, maybe because he just told me he was caught doing who knows what with a girl and was caught by my mother, which is awkward enough as is, but now knowing how involved he was with the town, it makes me want to run away, and I don't understand why.

"I'm sorry," he says, reaching over to grab my hand. I let him grab it and give him a smile, pushing my awkwardness away.

"It's fine, Ethan. It's in the past."

He grins at me. "You're the best." I smile back at him and revel in his compliment until I see who's over his shoulder and get the feeling I won't hold that title much longer.

"Incoming," I mutter as I squeeze his hand.

"Shit," he says, irritated when he sees Marie standing there with a few other girls. Judging by the looks on their faces, they obviously think the picture in front of them, i.e. Ethan and me, is distasteful. Either that or they all simultaneously ate lemons. *Let's go with that.*

"Ethan, wow! It's crazy to see you again!" Yes, so crazy. *Stalker whore.*

*Wow, I'm defensive. Shit.*

"Hey, nice to see you." *Yeah, he definitely doesn't mean that.* "How are you, Hannah?" *Hannah? The fuck?*

"I'm great, Ethan, yeah, great," says the blonde bimbo behind Marie, who shoots her a look like, *Back off, they're mine to torture.*

*whisk it all*

"Good. Well, we're gonna go get a beer."
"Oh! We'll come with you." *Super duper, Marie.* I can't wait to have three girls who obviously have a history with my boyfriend hang out and try to hit on him.

We all—yes, *all*—walk over to the keg that sits in a bucket of ice. There's a line, and as soon as I step in it, Carter Neilson—*yeah, I know people too*—comes over and steals Ethan away, leaving me with the gangbang squad. Don't worry, they're reverse gangbang, plus, it's voluntary.

I just gave myself the heebie-jeebies. Sorry, guys.

"So, Aveline." My name has never sounded worse than it does coming out of Marie's mouth. "You and Ethan seem to be together a lot these days."

*Ah, there you are Captain Obvious. I missed you.* "Yup, that's what happens when you date someone."

She laughs like I'm some cheap standup comedian. I mean, I can be though—funny AF. "You're adorable. Ethan is just biding his time, doll."

Ugh, I hate degrading pet names. "Uh huh." I step up in line, eager to fill my glass to the brim, guzzle the whole thing, and get the hell out of Dodge.

"I'm serious, hon." *Gag me.* "He's not really one to be tied down."

"You do realize he's been gone a long time, right? It is possible he's changed just a *little* since you guys hooked up."

"Aveline." Her serious tone makes me look her in the eye. If I didn't already know better, I would think she was about to be sincere. "We were engaged. We were supposed to be together after high school. It wasn't some casual hookup."

I don't even know how it happens, but suddenly I'm walking and I'm far away from the bonfire. I didn't reply

145

to Marie, having nothing intelligent to say. I didn't know about what she just told me, and I was not only embarrassed but also a bit pissed off. I'm not one to make a scene, though, so I walked away—away from her, the bonfire, and inevitably, Ethan.

I wish he had told me. Her having the one-up on me was embarrassing because he acted like she was nothing, and here she is telling me she's his—what, ex-fiancée? Is that for real?

I walk and walk until I'm practically back into town. The bonfire site is down at Danny Miller's place; it's always been there, as long as I can remember, and even though he's way past high school bonfire age, he still throws parties every summer.

It's a few miles to town and I'm shocked to find that I'm already back. We took Ethan's truck to the party, but luckily I have a key to the bakery on my house keys.

I wonder if he's noticed I'm gone by now. I know, I know, I'm a coward. I curse myself for leaving like that. I'm a freaking adult, but I'm acting like I'm in high school even though I didn't even act like this when I actually was in high school. Stupid.

I still can't get over how many people know Ethan so well. It makes me feel like I'm the outsider instead of the one who was born here, and I don't love the feeling. I have an itch to disappear, but I also don't want to leave Ethan.

I take a minute and let out a frustrated growl, shaking my arms and giving my foot a good stomp before I take in a deep breath.

There, much better.

Before I even unlock the bakery door, I turn around and start walking back. I have to at least confront him, need to understand why he didn't tell me about Marie.

I make it a mile before I see headlights coming my way and I raise my hand in a wave; likely I know the person who's in the truck. They slow the vehicle, and when they're close enough, I see why.

"Aveline! What the fuck are you doing?" Ethan jumps out and gets in my face. He's pissed, raging, and I've never seen him so mad. *Is it wrong that I like it?*

"What are you talking about? I'm walking back."

He grabs me and I think he's going to shake me, but he crushes me to him in a hard hug. "Fuck, Aveline. You scared the shit out of me!"

"I'm sorry, I just needed to think a little."

Ethan heaves a deep sigh like his world has done a 180 in the past hour. He looks to the sky, breathing deeply. "I thought that little dipshit Pete took you somewhere."

"Pete? Why would Pete do anything?"

"Because he has a major thing for you. He invited you on a fucking date tonight." That is kind of true.

"I don't like him, and he's not crazy enough to steal me away like that."

"You're right, because you're mine." Without another word he kisses me, pinning me to the side of his truck and guiding my arms around his shoulders. I melt right there, and too soon, it's over. "Why'd you leave?"

I mull over how I want to broach the topic of his ex-girlfriend—I'm sorry, *ex-fiancée*. "I had an interesting conversation with Marie."

He sighs again. "Great. What'd she have to say?" Ethan isn't big on sarcasm, but this sentence is laced with it.

"She was telling me how serious you two were in high school—ya know, probably trying to make me jealous. Unfortunately, it worked."

"We weren't that serious." He crinkles his eyebrows and I believe him, just like that, but...

"Really? So, you two weren't engaged?"

Ethan is surprised I know about this but not surprised to hear those words, not like I was. "Well..." His pause makes me drop my hands from his shoulders. It's not like it matters, but it still hurts that he didn't share it. "Hey." He grabs my arms and puts them back on his shoulders. "Listen, we dated on and off senior year, but I was always planning for the Marines and didn't want to have a girl-friend at home."

I nod to let him know I'm listening.

"Marie wanted to get married, that's true, but not for love. It was more like security." He runs a hand over his head like he hates the story. "She kind of proposed to me, but not traditionally. It was like 'consider this', but I said no. It wasn't fair to have a wife while being in the military, and certainly not one I wasn't even in love with. So, that's it."

"Seriously? Why not warn me though?" He stares at me, giving me the look he has when we've made love in his bed, the look he gives me when I surprise him with breakfast or when he shows up at the bakery unannounced. It's the look I haven't wanted to label yet out of fear.

"Honestly, when I'm with you, you're all I think about. I don't give a shit about anyone else—not anyone." My heart soars and takes a dive at the same time.

His confession both makes me fall and makes me want to run, but tonight, I take it and I fall.

"Take me home, Hart."

"Yes, ma'am."

# CHAPTER TWENTY-TWO

*Ethan*

"I LOVE YOU, Aveline."

My heart pounds in my chest, and I feel a bit like I'm hyperventilating—at least this is what I think it would feel like; I've never actually hyperventilated in my life. I stare at her and wait to see if she responds. She's in my favorite spot, right on my chest after another amazing night together.

Of course, she's sleeping. I just wanted to practice for when I really tell her, which will be soon.

After tonight's fiasco, she needs to know she's mine. She's my future, and I want nothing to do with Marie or any other girl. Also, she needs to know I'm never going to hold her back and she can do whatever she needs to do until she's ready to settle down.

I'm not an idiot; I know I'm putting myself on the line, but I know she's worth it. If she asked me to wait months for her to travel the world, I'd do so happily. If she asked me to go with her, I'd pack a bag. I think I'd do anything for this girl.

As a matter of fact, I almost think us traveling would make us stronger, would make our future together even more solid, and I fall asleep with a smile on my face as I consider the possibilities.

---

I crawl out of bed and let her sleep, knowing she has to be at the bakery this afternoon. I head for the kitchen and after starting a pot of coffee, I grab my laptop, which I haven't touched in weeks, to check my email.

The spam filters in and I delete everything I don't recognize until a few catch my eye. One is from a security company in California. I sent in a resume a couple months ago, and they want to have an interview with me. I ignore it since my plans have changed.

Another is from an email address I don't recognize, and it only contains one sentence.

*I'm watching and I'm waiting.*

*Okay, that's weird.* Someone has lost their damn mind sending that kind of spam. I delete that one too just as Aveline comes out of the bedroom then close the computer and stand to greet her. She doesn't say anything, just folds herself into my arms like I'm a safe place. I hope to stay that way for her.

"You're up early."

"Yeah, I've had a lot on my mind."

"Hm?" She mumbles into my chest, and I smile at her lack of alertness. Something I haven't been able to do in years is just block out the world.

"Yeah, but we can talk later. Let's get some coffee and then I have to go out and feed." She slowly pulls away and looks up at me like she knows what I'm thinking. I swear I can see her love for me in her eyes, and it puts me on top of a mountain.

⛰

Aveline left a couple of hours ago, but I can't drag myself back inside the house. The garage on the property is full of my uncle's collections from his years of being here; I'll probably end up finding dead animals or something equally unpleasant, and I'm not looking forward to it.

The garage is packed full to the brim, and I wonder how I never took notice of this space when I lived here. Boxes are stacked tall, and there are extra mattresses, a couch, chairs—you name it, it's in here.

I see a dining table I think would fit nicely in the house, and it's certainly a better option than the old one I've been using. When I lift some boxes off of it, I see a row of scratches on one end, and my breath catches when I realize what table this is. It was my parents' table.

The scratches are from when I was about five years old and I 'helped' my mom with dinner by cutting up some cucumbers on the table with a steak knife. My eyebrows come together as the pieces fall into place.

This stuff in here isn't random junk; it's my entire life—or my parents' entire life. I had no idea any of it was here, but once I start looking through one box, I can't stop and keep opening one after another.

When I left California after my parents passed, I only brought a bag with me and shipped a couple boxes, not wanting any memories of my past.

Now, looking through everything, finding my mom's clothes and our family photos, gratefulness for my uncle blooms in my chest and tears fall. I can't and don't care to stop them; this is a bigger moment than I was prepared for.

My memory and a few select photos I have on my old computer are all I have left of them—at least that's what I thought. Now, though, I realize I have every single photo we ever took.

I have pictures of my mom and me when I was first born, riding on my dad's shoulders, going to the zoo for the first time. There's me learning to ride my bike, camping, surfing, my first driving lesson—and that's where the pictures with my family end.

I spend hours sitting there, sorting through photos, and I don't even notice someone is here.

"Ethan?" Aveline's soft voice calls from outside. It's dark now and the light from the garage must have tipped her off. I wipe my eyes quickly and try to not look like I was weeping like a baby for the last few hours.

"Yeah!" I call to her. She pops up in the door a second later, a smile on her face, and then her eyes widen as she takes everything in.

"Wow, this is quite a lot of stuff." She picks up a blouse of my mom's from a box I opened and looks at me questioningly.

"It was my mother's." My confession makes her gasp. I nod my head, agreeing with the surprise she's feeling at the revelation. She covers her mouth with one hand and gently sets the shirt back down. Aveline walks over to me then, kneeling by where I'm sitting on an old milk crate.

"Oh my god." She reaches for a picture. It's my mom and me when I was only months old. My chubby cheeks are rosy, and I'm smiling at her. "She was beautiful, Ethan."

"She was." I take the picture from her and avoid eye contact, embarrassed to be so emotional.

"How'd you get all of their stuff?" Resting her hand on my knee, she waits patiently for my answer.

I blow out a heavy breath and run a hand over my head. "I don't even know. Carl must have had someone get it." I look at her wildly. "I had no idea it was here, all these years."

The thought makes me angry, makes me sad, and also makes me wonder why he never told me. "I almost sold this place without coming here, Aveline. I almost gave away my entire life. I can't believe it's all here."

"Oh, babe." She rubs my leg where her hand is and looks around. We don't speak for a while, marveling at the new discoveries. Eventually, she leads me into the house and makes me go take a shower while she makes dinner. I'm too exhausted to worry that she might burn the house down—it's just experience, not condescension.

When I come back out she has some pasta and sauce ready to go, and we sit in silence while we eat. I can tell she's treading lightly when she speaks up.

"I saw that table in there and if you're, ya know, comfortable with it, it would look great in here." She doesn't look at me as she speaks, but what she doesn't know is that's exactly what I needed to hear. "It would look nice, then you'd have something that was your family's. You can leave it in here, at least until you move. I don't know, sorry, I—"

"Aveline." I pause, waiting for her to look me in the eyes. When she does, I push my plate away and grab her hand. It's time for her to know her place—right next to me. "I love you."

I let the words hang in the air, knowing it will take her a minute to mull them over. I know internally she's freaking out—it's how she responds to scary and big moments—but I'm watching her, and this time she won't run. She'll stay, hopefully forever.

"Ethan..." Her eyes well with tears and my heart starts clenching painfully, waiting for rejection. "I love you, too."

I rise up out of my seat and pull her to stand, crushing my lips to hers. I wasn't expecting her to give me that answer, but I've never been so happy in my life.

This day has changed my life. Waking to find the love of my life was finally right in front of me, finding my entire past and memories just steps away, telling Aveline I love her—it's the best day ever.

We pull away and look into each other's eyes, and the euphoria catches us. We laugh, and we don't seem to be able to stop. I try to get a grip, and she slows her laughter. Her eyes reflect the happiness in mine; they're shiny with joyful tears.

"What does this mean?" she asks, a smile lighting up her face.

"It means we make it work." I move us to the couch to tell her my plans. "I'm not going to California."

She looks at me surprised. "You're not?"

"No way. I love you, so I stay with you."

"But..." She pauses, and I know where she's taking the conversation, but I need her to say it first. "I'm still taking my trip. I mean, I can't ask you to stay here and wait for me."

"I'll wait for you as long as it takes," I tell her honestly, because as much as it would suck, I would do it for her.

"Or..." I think she's caught on to what I've been hoping she'd ask. "You could come with me."

I smile at her, and I guide us until I have her under me, I take her lips with mine and we makeout like we're sixteen-year-old horn dogs. She pushes on me and I reluctantly pull back.

"Is that a yes?" she asks with a giggle.

"It's a hell yes. I'd follow you anywhere."

"Really?"

"Definitely."

# CHAPTER TWENTY-THREE

*Aveline*

IT'S HAPPENING AGAIN, you guys—I'm walking on clouds, nothing is in my way, and nothing could pull me off these magical fluff balls in the sky.

I'm in love.

It's not a feeling I'm used to. Okay, it's not a feeling I've ever felt before. I still can't believe I'm in love, and not only that, the man that loves me back? Yeah, he's pretty fucking awesome.

It's been a couple weeks since we said the words to each other, and not a single person was surprised. My mother was the one who caught on to everything. We were standing in the kitchen fixing dinner—something I've been neglecting a lot to spend nights at Ethan's—when she announced to everyone, "Aveline's in looooove." No, seriously, she said it just like that. Lucas replied with, "Shocker," and Grandpa asked when the wedding is, which is...um, not yet decided.

Not only do I get to revel in the fact that I am blissfully happy, we've also started talking about the trip too—our trip. It is no longer a solo trek but a couple's trip around the globe.

This made my mother ecstatic that I wasn't going to "get gangbanged in Europe." I get my sense of humor from her.

I thought having someone else to go with would put a damper on the things I wanted to do, that I wouldn't feel free to do everything I've dreamed of forever, but Ethan is fantastic in helping with the planning. Traveling is something he excels at.

For the first time, instead of dreading the end of summer, I am counting down the days until we finally get out of here.

Some time to ourselves without the prying eyes of Acton is going to be a totally different experience. We've discussed what it will be like to be in public and not run into someone who is trying to come between us, and it sounds divine.

Today is the Fourth of July and I am currently in my own little world, decorating celebratory cupcakes with red, white, and blue frosting. I am humming to the music coming from the stereo in the corner when my brother makes his appearance.

"Holy cow, you're alive," I declare. My brother has been aloof for the past few weeks; no one knows where he's been going. *Psh, boys.*

"Yeah, yeah, Mom gave me a whole lecture about it already so I don't need it again."

I hold my hands up in defense. "White flag, white flag," I say while laughing, because, dammit, I'm funny!

"Geez, your 'in love' attitude is very annoying."

I flick frosting at him and miss. "Sorry, grumpy. So where have you been going lately?"

"Oh, you know, I'm seeing a girl."

"Why are you yelling?" I ask—his voice went up several decibels on the last few words.

"No reason." I've never seen my baby brother blush, but as I live and breathe, it happens. So, being a good big sister, I call him on it. "No! I'm not blushing!"

"Seriously, stop yelling—you're going to scare the customers." I set the frosting down and face him, giving him my best serious face. "What is going on?"

He sighs and scratches his jaw—*wait, when did my brother grow scruff? The hell?* He mumbles something under his hand, and all I catch is "Kate."

"What? What about Kate?"

"I'm trying to make her jealous!" he whisper-yells, and I pull back and scrunch my eyebrows.

Leaning forward, I whisper back. "You like Kate?"

"Seriously, get out of your bubble! Even Ethan noticed." This is news to me, which makes me feel like a terrible sister. Even Ethan knew about this? Holy crap, time to hop off of my puffy cloud.

"I'm sorry. How long have you liked her?" I'm still whispering, trying to play fun, caring older sister instead of head-in-the-clouds sister.

"Uh, a long fucking time," he says flatly, staring at me like I'm an idiot.

Obviously, I've been in the bubble since long before Ethan came around if this has been happening for a while. I need to work on that, for real.

"And? What? She doesn't like you back?"

He chuckles. "Oh no, she likes me."

I'm confused. "Okay, so what's the problem exactly?"

"She's avoiding the inevitable, keeps playing the 'I need someone older' card. It's bullshit." He kicks at the ground and looks so beat up I can't help but feel sorry for him. I almost, *almost* want to be mad at Kate, but I'd rather her be blunt than lead him on—maybe not *so* blunt though.

"She means a lot to you?"

"Yeah." He sighs, picks up a cupcake, and shoves the entire thing in his mouth. *Damn.*

"Yeah, well that was sure attractive. You should've done that in front of her—she would be asking for a ring," I say sarcastically.

"Shuddup," he replies with a mouth full of cupcake.

The back door opens and Mom walks in, again with numerous bags in hand.

"Sheesh, what this time?" My tone is rather exasperated.

"It's for the booth!" she exclaims defensively.

Of course, it's a holiday, so obviously we had to throw another town party in the middle of the street. It's a good thing our town is not a big pass-through road because people would be so pissed that it was closed every other week.

There were only a few booths selected for the Fourth of July celebration, and we were 'lucky' enough to be one of them. I hate it. You get stuck at the booth while everyone else has fun. Lucas sometimes helps, and he does help set up, but he's usually nowhere to be found by the time the real party starts.

Kate, Mom, and I always run the booth in shifts. Last year, I took over for Kate for the one-hour shift and she never came back, claiming, "He was too hot *not* to dance with." Sure, okay. Mom is better but tends to get stuck talking to this person or that, and it's freaking annoying.

I don't usually care so much, but this year I have someone I want to see on the holidays. Go figure. Ethan offered to come sit with me, but I felt bad and told him to enjoy the party.

Still, I have a feeling he'll be sitting by me for most of the night because we're *in love*.

I'm so lame.

The party has been in full swing for a couple of hours now and Kate is already missing. She was here for like five minutes before something shiny caught her eye. Mom and I sell cupcakes so fast we're not sure how long we'll even be able to keep the booth open.

"I guess I should have made some more."

My mom looks so happy with the turnout. "No, it's not that! Look how many people aren't locals! We're on the map!"

I love seeing my mom happy. Losing my dad it hit her hard, but I've never seen a stronger woman. She pulled herself out of bed and made a life for herself. I wonder sometimes if she ever gets lonely, but she's never complained before.

Seeing this event—like most of the ones we take the cupcakes and baked goods to—make her this happy makes me feel so proud of her. It's going to be hard to not be around for a while when I leave, but I know my mom wants nothing but happiness for my brother and me. She's worked hard so we can do what we want with life.

I look forward to the future, to working in the bakery and hopefully becoming a wonderful mom then passing on her legacy. I hope someday I can make her proud in return.

"Where's Ethan?" Mom asks after selling another cupcake. She tucks the money away while I reach for my phone, and I frown when I see nothing there.

"I don't know, he was supposed to be here by now." I text him a simple *Where are you?* and then tuck my phone away to keep serving the cupcakes.

Two more hours pass and the fireworks go off, but Ethan never comes, never calls, never sends a text.

My phone pings and I jump on it only to find a message from a number I don't recognize. Attached is a picture. It's Ethan watching fireworks, but that's not what draws my attention. It's who he's with that catches my eye.

Marie.

*Motherfucker.*

# CHAPTER TWENTY-FOUR

*Ethan*

I HAVE NEVER been more uncomfortable in my entire life. This is the worst Fourth of July ever, and I can't blame anyone but myself. I'm standing here in a giant crowd of people who want to ask every question imaginable, and I think back to high school when I was an asshole and everyone left me alone except to praise me from afar.

*Those were the days.*

Not only is this bad, fucking Marie is here *again* and clinging like a suckerfish you can't extract. I don't hate people, but if anyone fell in that category, it would be her. She's nothing but trouble.

I mentally slap myself again for forgetting my phone, but I got caught up in the garage of stuff again and ran out of the house when I realized how late it was.

Aveline and I were supposed to watch the fireworks together, but when I got here, miraculously Marie found me, *oh thank goodness*—note the *strong* sarcasm. Still, I listened to her because she told me Aveline was already watching the fireworks with everyone else.

My eyes scan the crowd repeatedly, and I don't even look up at the lights in the sky; I only look for her. It's been twenty minutes and she's still not here, and I wonder if she's back at the booth.

I start to turn but Marie grabs my hand, trying to keep me there.

"Let go." My voice is hard, and I give her my best asshole look. She lets go, but she's not done.

"I don't understand, Ethan. Didn't you come back here for me?" This girl has lost her damn mind. She looks like she's about to cry, and I think its possible she's certifiable.

"You're insane. I came back for my uncle's house, and I ended up finding the love of my life. I'm sorry, Marie—it's not you, it's Aveline." I rip my hand and stalk away.

"You're making a big mistake! Big!" She's screaming behind me, but I don't even glance back. Marie is officially someone else's problem. I gotta find my girl.

The street that leads right through town is all but deserted, and I find her booth quickly. She's packing things away, and I notice her slouched posture. *Shit.*

"Ave!" I run up to her as quickly as my knee will let me. She turns toward me and sighs—not exactly a comforting welcome. "I'm so sorry, I lost track of time and then I forgot my phone so I couldn't call you."

She shrugs and continues to pack the odds and ends into giant plastic containers. "It's no big deal. I saw you got to see the fireworks."

My eyebrows pull together. "You saw me? How? I looked for you." I reach out for her hand and she lets me hold it. Her other hand pulls her phone out of her pocket and gives it to me. It's a picture of Marie and me watching the fireworks, and it looks intimate even though it isn't at all.

"What the hell? Who sent this to you?" I'm pissed. Some jackass is trying to cause a problem, and they picked the wrong guy to mess with.

"I don't know, I don't have their number." She looks tired, like she's just sick of anything Marie.

"It's not what it looks like. She told me you were watching the fireworks and I just went to look for you."

She nods her head. "I know. I mean, I believe you, I'm just sick of her shit, ya know."

I pull her into me and hug her. We need to just pack up our shit and leave this town so we can get away from the drama.

"Let me help get this stuff packed up then we'll go home, okay?" She mumbles her agreement in a relieved voice and directs me on what to help with.

She doesn't correct me when I say 'home', and I can't wait to make our home a permanent one.

Tonight, we're back at Aveline's grandparents' house for dinner again, and it's a perfect summer evening. The sun is low, but you can still see the mountains in all their glory. The sky is orange and blue, and the breeze is blowing; it's a picturesque Colorado evening. Lucas has a fire going in the fire pit while her grandpa grills and drinks a beer.

Aveline is dressed casually in a pair of jean shorts and a white tank. Her hair is flowing down over her shoulders, and I count my lucky stars for her. I'm sitting on a picnic table with Mrs. Montgomery, who insists I call her Belle.

"So, Aveline tells me you've decided to go on her trip with her." She gives me a small smile, a curious look in her eyes.

"Yes, well, she invited me." I sound cocky and quickly add, "Is that okay with you?"

She shrugs and chuckles. "I don't really get a choice, do I?"

"I would take your opinion into my thoughts, but you should know I've canceled any plans to go to California." I pause in the baring of my soul to my girlfriend's mother to decide how to say this, and I realize the saying 'honestly is the best policy' fits this situation. "I'm in love with her, Belle, and I don't want to plan a future without her in it."

She has a small smile on her face as she thinks over my confession. Her expression is contemplative, and she seems to be in a memory of her own. "You know, I was sixteen when I met Aveline's father." She pauses and takes a breath, her finger picking at the label on her beer. "It was love at first sight, at least it was for me. He didn't notice me at first, but I made him look any time I could. When he asked me on a date, it was the best day in my life. We got married when we were eighteen, and I had Aveline by the time I was twenty years old." She looks into my eyes again. "Sometimes, it just hits you out of nowhere, and the best decisions are made when you don't have to think about it too hard."

I nod in agreement and look over to see Aveline arguing

with Lucas over the fire, their grandma trying to pull them apart.

"I think you're great for her, Ethan. I'm very happy that you two are working this out." She grabs my hand and gives it a squeeze. "Aveline was telling me about your parents' stuff. I'm sorry you found it so suddenly like that, and I'm sorry about your parents. I don't think I ever told you that."

"Thank you." My voice cracks like an adolescent boy and I clear my throat. "I'm actually really happy I found it. It's something I thought I'd lost."

She nods her head in understanding. "I still have most of my husband's stuff, and it's hard to let it go. If you sell Carl's place and need to store it all somewhere, you let us know. We'd love to help."

I look at her in surprise. "Thank you, I really appreciate that."

Aveline finally comes and graces us with her presence. Sliding onto the bench beside me, she grabs my hand without thought, and I press my lips to her hand. She smiles at me and I want to take her away right then and there.

"What are you guys talking about?" She glances at her mom a bit suspiciously.

"Psh, what's that look for? I didn't say anything bad!" Belle holds her hands up defensively.

"She didn't. We were just talking about the future."

Aveline raises an eyebrow at me but doesn't comment. Lucas and her grandma come over to sit at the table with us, and soon we're talking about anything and everything, including the goings on in town and upcoming the parties and festivals. This town is notorious for their parties.

"What's the next thing on the calendar?" I ask, curious

about what Aveline will be dragging me to next. After the Fourth of July fiasco, we agreed we'd go to these events together or I'd just stay home. No more people butting into our shit.

"It's the beer fest, right?" she asks her mom, the family socialite.

"Now that's one I can get behind," I say.

"You took the words right out of my mouth," her grandpa says, coming up to the table with a plate full of burgers. This family goes all out for family dinners, and we dig in as soon as he sets them down. There is side after side spread out across the table and more food than you'd feed an entire party of people, but that is how they do it.

We talk about our upcoming trip and dive into the places we'll be going. Aveline is taking the lead because it is her dream, after all, but I've given my input when I have something I can help with. Most of the places we'll be going to will be new for both of us, and my excitement about having her to myself for so long grows every day, both literally and physically, if you get my gist.

The sun starts to fully set, and her grandparents say their good nights. The rest of us take our beers to the fire pit and sit around it in camping chairs.

"Hey, Luke, remember when Dad put this together for Grandpa?" Aveline asks him with a smile. He starts laughing and their mom joins them before Lucas fills in the blanks.

"That was great. When he lit it he used so much lighter fluid he nearly singed his eyebrows all the way off." They're all still laughing, and I chuckle along until something crosses my mind.

"Wasn't your dad a firefighter?" I ask Aveline, recalling

her mentioning something like that a while back.

"Yes." She and Lucas are laughing so hard tears are forming.

"He was a pyro, that man," Belle says, shaking her head. She's chuckling along, but her eyes stay on the fire. "He went right into his career after high school and loved every minute of it, but when he was off duty, he was the one setting the fires instead of putting them out." She shakes her head again and I catch her wiping under her eye, but I don't think Aveline sees it.

It's something else to witness someone still in love with her husband after so many years. It's plainly written on her face how in love she was with him, and I know his loss must have been hard for them to all take.

"Can you tell me more about him?" I ask, wanting to know this man who touched this family, wanting to understand who raised the woman I'm in love with. My question was for any one of them who is listening, and they continue telling stories about him.

His name was Jackson and he was a hero to the town, apparently, taking care of anyone who ever needed help even when it was the most inconvenient timing. Belle tells me the story of Aveline's birth and how he almost missed the whole thing because he was at a fire and saved some older woman from the top floor of a burning building. She says he still smelled like smoke when he finally made it to the hospital, but he was there when they welcomed Aveline into the world.

Aveline sniffs beside me and I can see the tears she's wiping away. I reach over and tuck her under my arm, wanting to comfort her. I know her pain, and it's not an easy thing to bear.

## whisk it all

"Ethan, will you tell us what your parents were like?" Belle asks. It's a heavy thing for me to answer. I haven't talked about them much since they died, but they all look at me, waiting patiently for me to tell them, and I realize these three are their own unit, their own family—one I want to be a part of.

So, I open my mouth and tell them all about my mom and dad.

# CHAPTER TWENTY-FIVE

*Aveline*

ETHAN OPENS UP about his family to mine, and I swear I fall more in love with him right then and there. We've spent the evening bonding, eating, drinking, and telling stories.

It's hard to hear stories about my dad, but I know it's something I want Ethan to share with us. The memories we have of him are something I want him to know. I want him to know I had an amazing dad. I truly believe he would have loved Ethan and would have loved us being together, and that makes me feel amazing.

My mom has been in a reminiscing mood tonight, laughing, crying, and just being genuinely open with us about dad. We've heard these stories before, but there's something different about tonight, a happier feeling in the air, and I think it has something to do with Ethan being here.

She asks Ethan to share about his parents, but I don't think he will. He and I have avoided the subject to a certain extent, and I've never wanted to push him to talk about something painful. I know sometimes it's hard to talk about my own dad.

"Well," Ethan starts, and I sit up a little in my seat, turning slightly into him to give him my full attention. "My mom was a doctor, an OB-GYN. She loved babies and loved seeing them come into the world." My mom and brother watch him, also giving him their attention. "She was always talking about how the world is so dark, but being a doctor and seeing these babies born was the light she needed. It was her passion from a young age. My parents met in college, and my dad got his business degree but ended up becoming a realtor. They were kind of a power couple." He chuckles.

Ethan keeps his gaze down as he talks, maybe thinking about what he wants to tell us. "I actually was going to be a doctor, too." This catches me by surprise. I grab his hand and he smiles at me. "I was pretty determined about it. We had my future planned, what school I'd try to get into, what specialty I would pursue. They supported me fully on anything I wanted to do. They never pushed, just guided." He takes a deep breath before continuing. "I was at a friend's house one night, my best friend back then. I stayed at his house and knew my parents were going to the movies, having a date like they did often. It was the next morning that I found out they got hit by a drunk driver and died instantly." He pinches the bridge of his nose and I rub my hand up and down his back. Tears are flowing down my cheeks for the pain he's feeling.

My mom is crying too, and Lucas looks sad for him, shaking his head.

"It was hard." His voice cracks and he takes a deep breath. "I never got to see them again, ya know. They were just gone."

We stay silent for a few minutes, allowing him time to get his thoughts together again. I'm mad for him, mad at the driver of that car, mad that his world was turned inside out. I'm mad I will never get to meet the people who raised the man I'm in love with. Life is so not fair.

"After that, I couldn't stay in Cali. My uncle came up for the funeral, and it was packed. You wouldn't believe how many people were devastated by their deaths. The day after, I packed a bag and came back with Uncle Carl. Let me tell you, my life was way different." He laughs, trying to break the tension.

"I'm so sorry, Ethan," my mom says, leaning forward to make eye contact with him. "That's not fair you had to deal with that so young."

"Yeah," he agrees solemnly. "I just wish I could have that family life back."

"Well, if it's any consolation, we are happy to have you in our family," my mom says, and I'm a bit surprised by her forwardness but grateful all the same. I squeeze him to me to convey how I feel.

"Yeah, man, I've always wanted a brother. You're not so bad, I guess."

"Lucas!" I scold. He's smirking like he's a funny little shit, and I want to smack him.

"Ha, thanks man." He tips his beer in my brother's direction with a smile like he's in on a joke with him.

I nudge Ethan's shoulder. "What happened to medical school?"

"It wasn't the same after Mom and Dad died," he says, his voice sad, and I feel for him. "I couldn't focus in school, barely passed my classes. I threw myself into football to release my anger and then didn't even hesitate when I joined the Marines. I figured if I couldn't honor Mom with a doctorate, I could honor our country."

My mom stands and walks over to us. "You've honored your mother well, honey." She squeezes his shoulder. "I'm heading to bed, kids. I'll see you." We say our goodbyes and Lucas follows not long after.

We stay there for a while just silently watching the flames, thinking over everything we revealed to each other and my family tonight.

"Will you come home with me?"

I smile at him lovingly. "Do you even have to ask?" He smiles back and leans over to kiss me. We put the fire out and when we're sure it's completely doused, we climb into his truck and head home.

*Home.*

"Aveline, pay attention!" My mother's voice snaps me out of my daze, my mind lost in the south of France with my boyfriend—or how I imagine it will be, anyway.

"Sorry," I mumble.

We're currently running through her newest recipes for the month, noting what was popular in the last few months, and going over the schedule of upcoming events. We have a big one we're doing all the way in downtown Denver. It's a huge deal, and Mom is going with a couple of extra assistants specifically hired for this one event.

"Where's your brain, my dear?" My mother is still looking over the schedule on the table we're sitting at in the front of the bakery, her glasses perched on the edge of her nose.

"Just stuff...thinking about the busy month," I reply, deflecting because I don't want to bring up my trip. Knowing I'm leaving her to run things all by herself is making me anxious, but she hasn't said anything herself.

"You're thinking about your trip, I bet. Excited?" She looks up at me then, her eyes warm with love.

"Well, yeah."

"What's wrong?" Mom sets her glasses on the table and grabs her cup of coffee, bringing it to her lips. She takes a sip and waits for me answer.

"I just...I don't know. I'm a little worried, leaving you to run the place by yourself." My admission makes me duck my head a little, ashamed about how selfish I feel.

"Oh honey, you don't need to worry about that." She grabs my hand and squeezes. "I have had plenty of time to prepare for you leaving. I'm going to find someone to temporarily help while you're gone, and then you'll come back and resume your duties. I want this for you—you need to have this experience." She pauses, taking a breath before looking at me again. "I want you to be sure about taking over the bakery. No regrets, got it?"

"Yeah. I love you, Mom." I lean over and hug her, feeling lighter after hearing her words.

"Ave!" Kate interrupts the moment and basically slams

into the chair across from us at the table. She has a grin a mile wide on her face, excitement is radiating off of her, and my eyes won't open wide enough to take it all in.

"Guess what?"

"You won the lottery?" I ask, actually being serious. Why else would she be so happy?

"No." She drags it out like I'm being ridiculous. "We are going out tonight!"

"Huh?"

"Oh, come on." She reaches across and grabs my hands. "I need a girls night and you're the only one I can think of that I can actually stand."

My mom chuckles at her and I scoff. "Gee, thanks a lot. Last resort much?"

"No! I just need someone mature to talk to who doesn't leave me for some guy."

"Well…" I hesitate because I was supposed to have dinner with Ethan.

"It probably wouldn't be a bad idea to spend some time with a girlfriend, Aveline," my mom says kindly, giving me a look like I don't really have a choice.

"I guess so." I give in, knowing it's not the end of the world to miss one day of seeing Ethan. The last four months have mainly consisted of seeing him, dreaming of him, and thinking of him.

"Yay! I'll pick you up at seven!" She scurries back behind the counter as a customer walks in.

"I'm glad you're doing that. Kate needs someone in her corner—she's having some trouble at home." Mom says it so nonchalantly I almost miss the seriousness of it.

"Like what? With her mom?" I ask. It's not a secret in town that her mom likes to get into bad situations, and I think it's why Kate seems to hang around us so much.

"Yeah. Lucas tries, but I think she's scared to get too close." Mom goes back to poring over the schedule, dismissing the subject.

I think about how infatuated my brother is with her and worry creeps into my brain. I know Kate would never purposefully hurt him, but maybe tonight is a good time to see where she's at mentally in regard to their relationship.

Detective Montgomery is on the case.

# CHAPTER TWENTY-SIX

*Aveline*

THE TOWN BAR isn't anything too special, and it's outdated. The booths vinyl seats are ripped and overused, the floor is covered with peanut shells, and it's an anaphylactic nightmare. The old jukebox has no music past 1989, and the owner is still the original guy from when my parents were teenagers. His son, who's my mom's age, runs it mostly, but the old man won't sign over the deed.

"I'm so happy you're able to leave your hot Marine to spend the night with me!" Kate bubbles again before taking a sip of her soda, and I laugh at her giddiness.

"Me too. It's been a long time since we've done this."

"I know. Man, I wish I could drink." She drinks some more and then grabs the bucket of peanuts. I watch her movements and realize she's nervous. *Time to figure out why, Watson.*

"So, what's been going on with you?"

Kate rolls her eyes, peanut half in her mouth as she breaks it apart. The image is so Kate—she's a goon and still looks gorgeous.

"Oh, you know, nothing special. I've been hiking a lot this summer, taking some pictures and stuff." She reaches into her purse and pulls her phone out. After tapping a few times, she hands it to me. It's open to her photos, and she tells me to scroll.

The photography is gorgeous, capturing the mountains, the scenery, and views from the tops of some mountain, though I can't tell where exactly. There are photos of a lake; it's beautiful and covered in flowers. I scroll to the next one.

"Holy shit," I say, surprised. On the screen are Kate and Lucas, kissing. I wordlessly hand the phone back, trying to gather my thoughts.

Kate looks at the image and her eyes widen. The soda she just drank spews all over the table and she coughs up the rest before catching her breath.

"So, how long has that been going on? Last I heard, you hated him." I give her my best mom look—problem is, I've never had to use one before and I'm not sure how effective it is.

"God, I thought I deleted that." Kate buries her face in her hands. "I'm sorry, Ave. I didn't want you to find out."

"Find out what exactly?"

"Well, we've been hanging out this summer, but I cut it off," she mumbles, looking ashamed. "I don't want to lead him on or hurt him."

"I don't understand—why would you hurt him?" I ask,

genuinely confused.

"I'm just...not good enough."

Shocked, I reach over and grab her hand. "That's absolutely ridiculous! Lucas adores you."

Her eyes tear up when I say that, and my heart breaks for her. "He deserves better, Ave." She takes a deep breath, and I'm out of things to say. I don't agree that she's not good enough, but I also don't know the extent of their relationship. The last time I gave any thought to it was Fourth of July when Lucas confided in me.

"Besides, I'm actually going to be leaving at the end of the summer." This time I'm the one choking on my drink, and my eyes widen with shock as I take in this new information.

"What? What are you talking about? Leaving where?"

"I got into a school in Denver, for photography." She blushes like she's embarrassed.

"Oh my god, Kate! That's amazing." I rush over to her side and hug her tight. She's needed to take a step like this for a while, and she finally has. I feel a rush of pride swell in my chest.

"Yeah, I'm pretty excited." She picks up her drink. "But I'll miss you guys." Her eyes cast over in sadness, something Kate doesn't show very often.

"We'll come visit, and I'll expect you to come home yourself every now and then."

We sit and chat about our futures, her leaving to live somewhere else, me going on a trip with my boyfriend. It all seems so surreal. Just months ago, we were working in a bakery, our dreams just out of reach, and now we're both getting ready to live them out.

Our giggles carry and the couple sitting at the bar

glances in our direction along with three other people. It makes us both realize how loud we're being and that we need to get out of here before we get kicked out.

Kate and I walk out the door arm in arm, and I wobble a little along the way, due to the four beers, I'm guessing. I'm not a big drinker, but Kate and I were having so much fun that I didn't even realize how quick I was drinking them.

"Aveline?" Someone calls my name from behind us and we stop—or more like stumble—to turn toward the voice.

It's a man, and he's tall and dark. His skin is bronzed like he lives in a tanning salon, only it looks natural; his hair is black, and his eyes are small. He looks almost scared, and his breathing is heavy.

"Are you Aveline?" He looks at me, cocking his head to the side, and it gives me chills—like creepy chills, not *holy shit you're hot* chills.

"Yes..." I say, my voice tilting in a question.

"Okay." He nods his head like I've confirmed everything for him then takes a step back and continues to walk backward until he's almost completely consumed by the dark.

"Good." Then he turns and runs away.

"Well, shit. That was scary," Kate says, tugging on my arm. "Let's get the hell out of here." We speed walk to her car, jumping in and locking the doors.

"Want to stay at my house tonight?" I ask, knowing I won't take no for an answer.

"Well, I sure as hell ain't driving home alone after that." Kate chuckles nervously. We're both so creeped out, we don't even speak until we finally make it all the way home, inside with the door dead-bolted.

I don't sleep well that night.

I have a hangover mixed with sleep deprivation, and it's horrible. My mouth is like cotton and my head is pounding like a drum. Something wet is on my face, and when I open my eyes, I see a black nose.

"Ugh, Stud," I moan, trying unsuccessfully to get myself out of bed, pushing him to the side. Chuckling from the floor, Kate sits up, her blonde hair sticking up everywhere, makeup smeared, somehow still looking beautiful.

"This is why I'm happy I can't drink because I know I would feel ten times worse than you do right now." She plops down onto my bed, sliding in between me and Stud and lets out a sigh. Rolling over, she cuddles me like we've been besties for years. Hell, she might just be my best friend.

"Ave—" Lucas bangs open the door, not the least bit concerned that I could be naked or something. *Seriously, no respect.* "Oh, shit. Hi, Kate." He awkwardly rubs his eyebrow.

"Hello, Luke."

Their formal responses freak me the hell out. For as long as I've been around these two, they've bickered like an old married couple. *Oh. Damn, I should've seen this sooner.*

"You guys want me to leave so you can make out?" I ask, and Lucas chokes on his spit right as Kate lets out a boisterous laugh. He reddens, and I just watch the scene unfold before me. Their relationship is not healthy.

"Um, Grams made breakfast." With that announcement, he hurries out the door, slamming it behind him.

"Well, that was fun."

"What the heck?" I say, because I don't know what else

to say. Kate doesn't answer me, though, instead standing from the bed and pulling me up with her. I groan again and squeeze my eyes shut, grabbing my head.

We walk down the stairs, me being a giant baby and clinging to Kate all the way down. The smell of coffee makes me pick up speed toward the kitchen.

"Oof, you look rough," says the voice of an angel, and I look up to see Ethan sitting at the table, a plate stacked with food in front of him.

"What are you doing here?" I stare at him in shock, mostly excited to see him but also horrified he's seeing me so miserable. He stands and peels me off of Kate, simultaneously rubbing Stud's ears by my side.

"Ugh, thank God! She weighs a million pounds."

"Hey!" I scold her. My glare goes unseen as she grabs her own seat and starts to pile food on her plate.

"Come on, baby."

"I'm not a baby," I answer even as I act like one. Ethan pours me coffee and juice, grabbing a bottle of Tylenol out of the cabinet like he lives here. No one even glances at him except for my mom.

"For heaven's sake, she can take care of herself. It's just a hangover." My mom chuckles at Ethan's affection but secretly I think she loves it; it's just like how my dad treated her.

"I don't know, did you sleep well? Because I didn't," Kate inquires.

"Not really, not after that guy." We exchange a glance.

"What guy?" Ethan asks, looking at me.

"Stormy Guy," Kate offers after swallowing some bacon.

"Stormy Guy?" I question.

"Yeah, he was stormy, all dark and mysterious—but

not like sexy mystery, like *I'd like to wear your skin* mystery, something I am not into."

"He was definitely not right."

"What the hell happened last night?" Ethan's voice is hard, his body tense.

"Language," Grandma says sternly. Her eyes haven't even looked at me the entire time, her newspaper far more interesting to her.

"Not much, really, but as we were leaving, some guy asked if I was Aveline." I mull over that, only now wondering why he needed to know who I was.

"What?" Ethan whispers. "What else?"

"That was all," Kate tells him. "He just confirmed she was Aveline and ran away." She looks at Lucas, who looks as concerned as Ethan. "He literally ran—it was crazy."

They drop it then, but I know Ethan is still stewing over what happened. It's not like there aren't crazy people in Acton—I mean, there's always someone—but it was a little strange that he knew my name. Maybe he's been to the bakery; surely my name is on something there somewhere.

We finish breakfast in silence, a tension now filling the air between Ethan and me, and I don't know what to do about it.

# CHAPTER TWENTY-SEVEN

*Aveline*

I'VE FINALLY BEEN talked into a camping trip. It's not like I am opposed to camping technically, and when Kate insisted she wanted to go, I couldn't turn her down.

Ethan is happy about the trip; he loves being outside, so this is no surprise. I'll admit, lying out in the wilderness is much more appealing when I have him to look forward to.

Unfortunately, that is the only silver lining to the idea of camping.

Don't get me wrong, I don't hate it; it's more like it makes me itchy, makes me achy, makes me wish to all that is holy that they would make outdoor showering a thing.

I hate being dirty. Plus, Ethan hasn't experienced stinky Aveline yet, and he is about to get the full experience.

I guess what is really weighing on me is the fact that this is the final test, the test that will show us if we are going to be able to tolerate each other even at our absolute worst.

"Are you ready, babe? They'll be here any minute," Ethan says, peeking his head around the corner of the door frame. I am currently standing by the bed staring into the duffel bag on the bed, my things haphazardly thrown about, deciding what is necessary for our long weekend in the mountains.

"Yeah, yeah, almost ready," I answer distractedly. Pursing my lips, I add some tank tops into the bag. *Maybe just one more...*

"Hon, you're not even packed," Ethan points out as he walks over to the bed to see what I've decided needs to come with us.

"Sure I am, I just have to decide," I say like it's obvious.

"You really think you're going to find somewhere to shave while we're in the middle of nowhere camping?" He picks up the two razors I have on the bed near the toiletry bag. I open my mouth, but he shakes his head and throws them to the side. "No, you won't. That's a want, not a need."

Frowning, I watch as he starts to pack my bag for me, and I'm not exactly thrilled about which hygiene products he has decided I'm not allowed to take.

"No, no way. Put that back." I snatch away the deodorant and throw it in the bag. "I can go without a lot of things, but deodorant is a hard limit for me."

He chuckles. "You realize in the military we go without showers for weeks at a time, right? I can handle B.O."

I raise an eyebrow at him. "Uh huh. Well, none of them were your girlfriend. Plus, I have options. You didn't."

He raises his hands and concedes. I finish loading my

duffel with some clothes and fresh underwear. When I'm satisfied, I zip it up, and Ethan grabs it before I can then walks it out to his truck.

Lucas and Kate pull up in her little car, and I smile at how happy they look. I'm also happy—happy they've worked out their crap and are finally acting like adults.

We load our bags and coolers, and I grab Stud and load him in. I wouldn't be going without this dog. We pile in around him and start heading into the mountains to the campsite we reserved for the weekend. It's apparently one of Kate's favorites, and it still surprises me that she is so into camping considering how girly she tends to be.

When we pull into the site a couple hours later, the area is nearly full. The height of camping season is in full swing, and I'm surprised we even got such a nice spot.

The guys immediately start setting up the tents, and I try not to cringe at the fact that Lucas and Kate only brought one, although I imagine Lucas feels the same way about our sleeping situation.

I help Ethan finish setting up and unroll our sleeping bags, spreading them out in the tent. Seeing our stuff set up in there makes me almost feel excited for this camping trip—almost.

"Who's up for a hike?" Kate asks the group once our stuff is all set. I look at Ethan and he nods his head. I never know when he hits his limit with his knee, but he never complains, and I take that to mean he doesn't want me bringing it up all the time.

We set off on one of the shorter hikes so it won't take us too long; the longer one we plan to tackle tomorrow.

Kate takes the lead, camera in tow and snapping pictures left and right. Lucas helps her with equipment she needs, and I watch how they interact with each other. It's obvious they've done this a time or two.

I'm ahead of Ethan, urging Stud to pull me up the hill, and I take in the gorgeous trees and plants all around. Everything is in full bloom, summer at its peak, and the mountains are beautiful. I glance behind me and see Ethan is right on my trail, keeping up without losing his breath.

I'm already panting on my way up this mountain, and I have to restrain myself from asking when we'll turn around. We've only been hiking for about thirty minutes.

We pass several other hikers, all walking with smiles on their faces, having the time of their lives. When they greet us, I pant out an incomprehensible salutation or just throw my hand up at them.

I stop for a minute to catch my breath and Ethan steps up, wrapping his arm around my waist. "You doing okay, babe?"

"Oh, psh, yeah!" I exhale heavily. "I'm doing great." Looking at Ethan, I see he has a sheen of sweat on his forehead. "Are you?"

"Yeah." He reaches down to rub his knee and looks at it. "I'm doing good, actually. I'm not feeling sore yet."

I nod at him and we continue, hurrying to catch up with Lucas and Kate.

We reach the end of the trail not too long after that.

Standing at the top, looking out on the view that's revealed to us is breathtaking, and I imagine a house being built right here on the edge of the mountain. If only.

We get back to the campsite and go about making some dinner. With the fire going and the conversation flowing, the evening is turning out to be one of the best of the summer, and I find myself hoping we'll get to do this again.

It's nice to get away from town and responsibility, even if it's only for a couple days.

This whole weekend is like a trial run for Ethan and me for our trip this fall, and it's fun to plan with him instead of just planning for myself.

He hands me a plate and we all dig into the first meal we brought. We all pitched in for the food so it wouldn't be too expensive for anyone.

"So, Aveline, how do you like the trip so far?" Kate asks, giving me a smirk.

"Oh, well, I've only had to pee behind a tree once, so I'd call that a win." Everyone laughs, and we continue our talk. I throw Stud a hotdog I cooked for him and Lucas rolls his eyes. I stick my tongue out at him.

"When do you leave for school, Kate?" Ethan asks, keeping the conversation going.

"Right at the end of August, early September at the latest. My classes start in September, and I want to get settled into my dorm first." She beams with excitement and my eyes find Lucas'; he doesn't seem all that upset about her leaving.

We chat a while longer and then turn in for the night. Unfortunately, I have to pee again.

I'm clutching the toilet paper to my chest and peeking out the tent's zipper door.

"What's wrong, babe?" Ethan asks, giving me a peculiar look.

"I'm scared," I admit in the dark, the only light coming

from the small battery-operated lamp we have in the middle of us. "I have to pee, but it's so dark."

He chuckles and gets into a crouch in front of me. "Would you feel better if I came with you?"

I nod and he smiles. I know in his head he's making fun of me, but he doesn't voice anything out loud. We go behind the tent and crawl around a couple of trees, Ethan holding Stud's leash—I'm pretty sure he could eat a bear if I needed him too. When I find one big enough to hide my embarrassment, I tell Ethan to turn around.

It's so quiet out here that when I try to pee, I can't seem to make myself break the silence. After a few minutes, Ethan asks if I'm okay.

"It's too quiet," I reply.

"Too quiet?" he asks, confusion in his tone.

"Yeah." I hesitate. Then, like a gift from heaven, I hear a voice singing. It's Ethan.

"It takes two to make a thing go right, it takes two to make it out of sight."

I can't stop laughing, and the result is relief. When I return to his side, I smile and give him a kiss. "Thank you."

He laughs. "Saw it in a movie." We walk back to our campsite and cuddle in the sleeping bags. We nestle close, my cold to his hot. It doesn't take long for me to fall asleep, and my final thought is that I can't wait for our trip.

# CHAPTER TWENTY-EIGHT

*Ethan*

I HATE HAVING good intuition sometimes. It's a real pain in the ass; like, can't I just have a normal reaction to things? Can't I, just for once, let things go?

The answer is no. I can't let things go, not when my gut says something bad is going to happen. In the military, it was a great gift to have; people trusted it even. I could hold us back from getting our heads shot off, and I could map out routes that wouldn't end in explosions.

Until that last one, that is.

That's why, this time, I'm fully listening to my gut, and my gut says, *Don't let Aveline out of your sight.*

I don't. It's almost August, and she and her mom are busy with the business, trying to get everything ready for our departure. It's hectic and she runs back and forth from the bakery to her house to my house to school. The girl has no breaks, and me following her around is getting on her nerves.

I can't bring up the fact that I'm scared someone is messing with her. The man she encountered really unnerved me, and I couldn't stand it if something happened to her because I wasn't cautious.

Today, she's at the bakery, a normal baking day like the beginning of summer. Her mother needed to get things ready for an upcoming event in Denver, and Aveline has to take over all the bakery needs.

I'm in the garage, getting my parents stuff organized so I can have it moved over to Belle's house. I had the house put on the market a couple of weeks ago, and we are already working on someone's offer. It's enough to give me cash to travel for a while before I need to find a job, and I'm relieved to have it.

It's been a bit bittersweet to sell my uncle's house. It was a place I was forced to grow up in, somewhere I hated to be at the time but now am glad to have had. I wasn't grateful enough for my uncle, and I'll always regret not telling him I loved him.

My emotions while going through their stuff and selling this house are some I'm not used to dealing with, but I'm excited for the future.

The gravel in my driveway crunches and I recognize the sound of Aveline's Jeep. I glance at my watch with a frown—she wasn't supposed to be off work yet. I walk out of the garage, a smile on my face as I see her move quickly toward me.

My smile disappears when I see the pissed-off look on

her face. She's holding a piece of paper and she slams it into my chest.

"I've had it!" she yells, throwing her arms up in the air. Confused, I read the note: *You won't last. I'll make sure of it.*

"What? Who gave this to you?" I curl my hand into a fist, crumpling the paper.

"Who do you think? It has to be Marie!" Aveline starts pacing, frustration clear on her face. "Why is she so set on pissing me off?"

"I don't know," I answer, but then I pause. I look at the note again and think. When realization hits me, I hold my breath, trying to stave off the panic that is settling in my chest. When I can breathe normally, I pull Aveline into me.

"I'm going to take care of this, okay?" I look her in the eyes and kiss her hard.

"What are you going to do?" she asks, gaze locked on mine.

"Don't worry about it, okay? Just keep getting everything organized and I'll call you when things are taken care of."

Aveline closes her eyes and takes a deep breath. When she releases it, she opens her eyes and smiles at me again. "Okay." We walk to her Jeep and she gets back in. Rolling down her window, she leans out. "I can't wait to leave the drama behind." I kiss her again, hoping I can save our trip from the truth I just discovered.

Aveline waves out her window as she pulls back out onto the highway, leaving me to clean up the mess.

I should have seen the signs earlier, should have realized what is going on. The emails, the picture from Fourth of July, the guy at the bar, and now the note—I wish it were as easy as an ex-girlfriend trying to get back at me for ripping her heart out or someone who realized they missed their chance with Aveline, but it's not that simple.

It rarely ever is.

Realistically, I could have figured this out right after Aveline told me about the guy at the bar. She described him perfectly, right down to his odd demeanor. He knows who she is, and he is going to use her to get back at me.

David is finally collecting on my life for Brad's, and I need to stop him before anyone gets hurt.

Aveline left hours ago and sent me a couple of texts, but I needed to figure out David before I explained and scared her with something I could handle without involving her.

Searching my email's inbox, I find the three emails I've received from anonymous senders over the last couple of months. The distance between each one is unnerving; he's been planning whatever he's going to do for a while.

Each email is a threat to me. They're not anything specific, which is why it didn't unnerve me before, but when everything is added up, it all makes sense.

Picking up my phone, I make a call to someone I haven't talked to since we both got out.

The ringing on the line continues a couple of times before he answers. "Walters."

"Walters, Hart."

"Hey buddy, what's going on with you?" Greg Walters is someone you want on your side. He is a genius with tech and can find anything you're looking for. The military loved having his skills working for them, but he got out to be a contractor, ready for more money.

"I'm okay. I've got a job for you." I go into detail about what's going on with David. He knew him and Brad as well, being in the same unit as us. So, hearing about him coming after me gets a fire lit under him, and he promises to get me information ASAP.

As I hang up, I get another call, this one from the realtor I recently hired to sell Uncle Carl's farm. Her name is Theresa and she is literally the only realtor in Acton.

"Ethan, we've got a great offer!"

"A new one? That was quick," I say, looking around the house at everything I still need to get packed up.

"Your uncle's property is very desirable, being in a great location with a great setup. This couple wants to get into it soon."

"Full offer?"

"Full offer, and to show their good faith, they want to cover the realtor fees. This is an excellent offer, Ethan."

I let out a long sigh. With everything going on with David, I don't know how I'm going to get everything packed up, but then again, I need everything to be done before Aveline and I leave.

"Okay, accept. Let's get this done." We agree on a time to meet to get the paperwork together, and I make a call to Aveline's mom, hoping she's still willing to store my stuff. She agrees easily, telling me to bring whatever I need, but I don't think she understands how much junk I've got.

Once I hang up, I get to work. I've only got four weeks to get everything in storage and find the asshole who's threatening me and my girl.

I decide to go ahead and bring a load over to her house, so I pack up as many boxes into the back of my truck as possible and head over. Lucas meets me at their extra barn and helps me unload. We talk shit while we work, and I realize how much like Aveline he is—he cuts himself three times and trips over his feet more times than I can count. I shake my head and wave goodbye after the last of it is unloaded.

I work for hours, going through my shit and Uncle Carl's, packing what I want to keep and starting a giant trash pile. The work eventually gets the best of me and I fall asleep, crashing out quickly. I don't eat, I don't shower, and I don't see that I missed a call from Aveline.

# CHAPTER TWENTY-NINE

*Aveline*

I MESSED UP. I got too jealous and too pissy and I scared him off. Yes, I said 'pissy'—got a problem with it? I growl in frustration as I smudge *another* cupcake in my hasty anger.

After I left Ethan's house the other day, I tried calling him that night but he never answered. When I heard he'd been at my house, I wondered why he never came inside; I was there. The day after that, I called again, and no answer. I texted him once, the only amount I was allowing myself per day, but he never answered that either.

It's been four days of no communication, no texts or calls, no random bakery drop-bys. My mother saw him once when he dropped more things off at the house, but I was in class.

I get the feeling I'm getting ghosted, and I don't know why. I didn't think I came on too strong about the whole Marie thing, but maybe he felt differently about it than I did.

Maybe he thinks I am a jealous, crazy girlfriend who won't ever stop, but really I was just fed up after receiving that note.

I'd gone into the bakery that morning happy as could be. My life was shaping up so well that it could have been a novel. The day was going by quickly with all the work we'd acquired for the end of summer, and it was a nuthouse in the kitchen.

Kate came back and handed me a note with a secret smile on her face. "Someone dropped this off for you. Seems you have an admirer."

I smiled, thinking she was just talking about Ethan, which wouldn't be completely weird—he's a romantic at heart.

When I opened the note that had my name scrawled across the front, my smile slipped from my face. Whoever sent this wasn't some admirer who wanted to be with me; it was someone who wanted to take away my happiness.

It pissed me off. I saw red as I ripped off my apron and threw it on the ground. I yelled at Sunny, our chef, saying I'd be back, and then I went to Ethan's.

I don't know what came over me that day, but I was so mad someone was so hell-bent on breaking us up that they'd threaten me in writing. It must have been my desire to stay with Ethan, to keep him in my life, and I didn't want to imagine what would happen if she were to succeed.

Now, though—now I wish I had reined in my anger,

because I'm pretty sure my boyfriend is no longer my boyfriend.

My eyes well with tears as I think about what I've screwed up. Kate comes into the back with a hot coffee in her hand, and her eyes hold sympathy. She's been my confidant throughout the last few days, allowing me to vent and open up about everything.

"How are you doing?" she asks, her eyes scanning my mess of cupcakes, white frosting smeared over my workspace.

"Oh..." I let out a shaky sigh. "You know."

She cocks her head, her smile tipped with pity. I hate having people looking at me like that. She and Lucas are the only ones aware of the fact that Ethan and I aren't even talking. I can't stand my mom or grandparents knowing about this; they grew to love him and are storing his stuff now, so the less they know, the better.

"Yeah, I get it. Hey, let's do dinner again tonight."

I pause, wanting to turn her down; I hate the idea of going out. All I want to do is go home with some ice cream and hide under my covers. *I'm pathetic.*

"It'll be fun!" Her cheery attitude is slightly infectious, and I open my mouth to respond just as the door opens.

"What will be fun?" Lucas asks, looking at Kate like she hung the moon. I don't even want to get into those two right now. My brain can't handle it.

"I'm trying to get Ave to have dinner with me," she says, looking away.

"Oh, that's a good idea. I'll join." Lucas' gaze lingers on her before he turns to me and nudges me in the shoulder. "Hey, I saw Ethan this morning."

My eyes shoot to his. "You did?"

He nods. "Yeah, he brought more stuff to the house. Didn't talk to him much, and per your request, I didn't talk about you."

I swallow the lump that's forming in my throat, trying to hold down tears. This jerk blows me off and then still uses my family's property to store his shit?

"How did he look?" I can't help but ask.

"Honestly?" I nod. "He looks pretty beat up, like he hasn't been sleeping much. I asked if he was okay, but he just said he was trying to get his shit together."

I shake my head. What does that even mean? Get his shit together so he can leave me?

I sigh, turning back to my disasterous cupcakes. "I've got to get back to work."

They both stare for a minute before Kate speaks up. "Dinner, please?" Her expression is sad, and I remind myself we'll be going our separate ways in a few short weeks.

"Okay."

I stare in the mirror for a full ten minutes wondering why the hell I care about how I look. I don't have anyone to dress up for—not anymore.

The jeans and white tank are going to have to do it because I've lost all energy. Nothing seems to get me excited the last few days. Lucas knocks on my door to tell me it's time to leave, and I grab my bag then trudge down the stairs.

We're loading into his truck when another familiar one starts to pull through on the road that leads down from the barn, heading back toward the highway. I pause, my hand on the door handle and my eyes pinned to the other vehicle.

It slows to a stop and Ethan steps out. I don't move for a minute but then decide the inevitable will happen.

Ethan meets me halfway and I can feel Lucas move in a little closer, my protective little brother. Ethan does look tired, like he hasn't really slept for a few days. The scruff on his face is the longest I've ever seen it, and I take in his dirty clothes all the way down to his scuffed boots.

"Hey." His voice is hoarse like he hasn't spoken in a while.

I cross my arms defensively, literally feeling myself soften in his presence. *I'm mad at him, dammit!* "Hi."

"How are you doing? You okay?" His eyes are wide, taking me in; his voice, though, is condescending, like *Are you okay after the big bad Marine broke your poor little heart?* Ugh, I could smack him.

I scoff at him, my grin sarcastic. "I'm doing just fine. How about you? Got everything you need from us?" I know I'm being snarky, but I couldn't care less. He's been treating me like shit, and it's time he feels like it.

"Aveline—" he starts, reaching for me. I take a step back.

"No, I'm done." I turn and jump into Lucas' truck, slamming the door and locking it. I'm done, I'm pissed, I want to scream, and I want to cry. What I don't want is to listen to his excuses—not anymore.

---

The restaurant is packed, everyone and their mother are in here, and I'm sloshed. I don't remember ordering the first margarita, or the second, or the third—but I sure did drink them.

I blame Kate.

After I told her what happened at the house, she immediately waved the waitress down and started ordering the entire menu. I'm not even joking, you couldn't tell what color the table is if you tried.

Kate is telling me about her experience going for a hike by herself, to which Lucas replied saying he told her he would've gone with her, but the story has me snorting margarita through my nose. I'm starting to think I should get my sinuses checked because it freaking burns to have that shoot through there.

"I'm not kidding! I would have sworn on the Bible that it was a bear!" We're all laughing so hard tears are streaming down our faces.

"But it was a dog?" I barely get the words out.

"A big fucking dog! I'm talking behemoth!" She's laughing so hard she knocks her drink off the table and it goes everywhere.

"I'm sorry," she says solemnly to the nice young waiter who's serving us. I think he's officially annoyed at the drunk group in the corner, except I'm the only one drinking.

I smile, finally feeling like myself again. I pushed Ethan out of my head the moment we walked into the restaurant, and I finally have some peace of mind. I'm still pissed, but I am at least able to enjoy a night with my friends.

Just when I think I might return to normal, karma slaps me right across the face.

"Hi, Aveline." At the sound of Marie's whiny-ass voice, my eyes roll so hard they hurt. She's wearing a skintight dress, her hooker boots go up over her knees, and her red lipstick is perfectly placed on her model-like looks. Dammit, I hate that she's pretty. Too bad she's a terrible person.

"Marie. What can I do for you?" I bring my margarita to my lips and take a hefty swallow.

"I just wanted to let you know how sorry I am. I know how you cared for Ethan."

"Oh yeah?" I ask, because I know she's not the least bit sorry. "And how would you know how much I cared about him?" It's not surprising she thinks she knows this; half the town was up in our business the moment the two of us met. It was why I was so excited to be alone with him in Europe.

"Well, we were talking, and he feels bad about everything that's happened."

Her words make my blood boil. They were talking—what does that mean? Does it mean she finally succeeded? Is he that much of an idiot?

Kate scoffs. "Shut the fuck up, Marie. You two didn't talk about shit." She stands from the table, and Lucas and I watch in surprise and amazement as she towers over tiny Marie. *When did Kate get so tall?* "If you don't leave Aveline alone, I'll rip your fake lips right off your face and feed them to my cat. Got it?"

Marie's eyes widen and she stumbles back a step, stammering out an incoherent sentence before she runs away from our table.

"Shit, now I love you even more," Lucas says with awe in his voice.

"Yeah, me too," I say to her.

Kate giggles and takes a drink of her fresh iced tea. "That bitch has no boundaries, and she needed to be put down." She sighs. "Don't believe the shit she said—she's obviously very jealous of you."

More than likely, Marie is a big fat liar, but I can't help but wonder if any of it is true. It's too bad I'll never know, because Ethan is also a liar, and that hurts worst of all.

# CHAPTER THIRTY

*Ethan*

SURVEILLANCE HAS NEVER been my strong suit—the waiting around for countless hours, the inaction of the job itself, never knowing when I'll be able to move from one spot to the next.

I'm lucky I learned how to have patience in the military, because otherwise I would have lost my mind a long time ago.

I'm so sick of this shit. I shouldn't have to fucking stalk a former teammate of mine. It's been two weeks since the note, two weeks since Aveline has really talked to me.

The last image I have of her in my brain haunts me day and night, and I'm worried the longer I don't answer her about what's going on, the slimmer the chance I have of getting her back.

If I weren't stalking David, if I didn't have to take care of this problem, we would be packing for the trip we're supposed to start in two weeks. Instead, I must deal with a psycho who won't answer me, who's hiding, and who's threatening me and my girlfriend.

Just thinking about it makes my blood boil.

Walters worked for hours tracking David down—the little fucker was sneaky, using only cash at a shitty pay-by-the-hour motel outside of town.

It took him twelve days to slip up and use a credit card at an ATM near the motel, and it was easy enough to put two and two together. So, now I sit here in my truck, waiting. I've been here all night, waiting for him to move, to do anything, but so far, nothing.

I sent him an email back to the anonymous address he used, but it came back as undeliverable.

So, I bided my time, waited until Walters found something. While I waited, I packed, and I had everything I didn't want hauled off to the dump then took the rest to Belle's house. If she knows anything about Aveline and me, she didn't show it. I almost wish I could talk to her about it, because right now I'm completely alone.

The sun rises, and I hope I can end this today. A door opens at the far corner of the motel and David walks out. His head is down, and he has a bag strapped to him. He gets into a beater car and gets onto the highway, heading toward Acton.

I follow him with a few cars between us, hoping to not be seen. He exits and I slow down, waiting for him to turn so I can follow him. David heads out onto the road that takes you right into the heart of Acton.

My heart rate kicks up a notch and I wonder if Aveline is working today, but he drives past the bakery, pulling into a spot in front of the hardware store.

Now he's wearing a ball cap and sunglasses, the brim pulled low so you can't really see his face. I wait across the street for him to enter the store, and when he does, I exit my truck and run inside.

I slow down when I get to the door and swing it open; the bell dings but there's no one in the front. I forget the name of the old man who owns the store, but I'm glad to see he's not here right now.

Slowly, I walk down the aisles, searching each one. My hand reaches to my back, ready to pull my piece if necessary. I don't know how far gone David is, but the fact that he's here and has been, the fact that he's at the hardware store now means he's not going down without some sort of fight.

I reach the aisle that has ropes and chains and curse under my breath, having an idea of what he's going to do with it. My hand is fully grasping my gun now, pulling it out of its holster and ready to get this guy caught.

He's grasping a chain in his left hand and pulls it tight with his right, like he's testing the strength. I inch out a little closer, deciding on my next move, and then a guy with a nametag comes out of the next aisle, striding up to me with a smile on his face.

"Hi, how can I assist you today?" The employee approaches me as I turn toward David, who he bolts out the front door when he sees me.

"Shit!" I run, hoping I can tag him before he's gone, but he's already in his car. I get to my truck and throw my door open, peeling out of my spot before it's even shut.

I can barely see his piece-of-shit car up the street when a fucking school attendant with a stop sign stops me mid-chase. *Motherfucker.*

David's gone.

---

As I suspected, David checked out of the motel he was in and is now in hiding once again. Luck isn't on my side this time around.

I make a call to Walters, asking him to start a whole new search, and then I go home and pour myself a drink. I'm so done with his game. All I want to do is be with Aveline. I want to escape this nightmare I'm living and get her in my arms again.

Every bit of this situation pisses me off, but maybe this is my punishment for hitting the IED. Maybe God has finally had enough of me and the consequence is for me to suffer, for my life to be the hell I've been living in recently.

I think back to being in the military with him. We were never enemies; in fact, our unit was quite close, though he and Brad were definitely the closest of the group. I know they came from the same hometown and had a friendship before getting into the Marines, so in a way I can understand his pain, his sadness, and his anger. I get that he's pissed, but I also understand that's he's lost his damn mind. He needs help, and I intend to make that happen for him.

Even though he's trying to hurt me, he's just going to continue to hurt himself if he stays on this path of revenge he's been on.

My mind is lost when my computer pings an alert that

I've received a new email. I sit up and tap the track pad, watching as the bright screens illuminates the dark room. I hadn't even noticed it's night, too caught up in my thoughts.

The email is from David, the same anonymous address as before, and I eagerly click to open it.

The subject line is blank. The email itself contains a picture, and the words underneath say: *There's more than one way to get what I need. Can't wait to put my new toys to use.*

The picture itself is dark, the light from a lamp lighting up the items on a standard hotel room desk. On the desk, I see rope, chains, and pliers. I sigh and scrub my hands over my head. The panic I feel is extreme, and I don't know what I'm supposed to do.

I look at the clock and try to remember what the hell day of the week it is. It's just past nine now on Friday, meaning Aveline isn't at school and more than likely has been home for a while now. My relief is palpable.

Sighing, I click reply. I don't think this email will go through, but I have to try to get ahold of him. Then, I have to spend the night trying to find out where this fucker's gonna be.

*David, meet me somewhere and I'll do whatever you want.*

No demands, no questions, just a straight resignation. Of course, I'll probably kick his ass, but he doesn't need to know that.

I check my phone to make sure Walters hasn't said anything, and I'm surprised when I find a text from Aveline. I open it without even thinking about it. I haven't talked to her in forever, and my hope that she can wait just a little longer is strong.

*Ethan, I know you probably don't care that I'm sending this, but I can't let myself wonder anymore, so this is my last text to you. I'm sorry I wasn't good enough for you, but I'm good enough for me. I hope you have a nice life. Good luck. – Aveline*

My heart breaks when I read her words. She's giving me up, and I don't blame her at all. I've been an asshole these last few weeks, trying to fix something that will affect her without involving her.

She needs to know what's going on. She has to understand why I'm doing this, and it's time to bring her into it.

With David's threat hanging over my head, I get in my truck and do a quick search of hotels within fifty miles. I'll search all night for him and then in the morning, whether I've found him or not, I'll go to Aveline and tell her everything.

# CHAPTER THIRTY-ONE

*Aveline*

THE CITY IS so much different than where we live, and for the first time in my life, I wonder what it would be like if I lived here. It's gorgeous. The venue for the event we're participating in is right by Coors Field, home of Rockies baseball.

It's alive, the people and the animals, the trees. The buildings are all done in different styles of architecture, everyone is out and about on this gorgeous Saturday, and I can't help the small smile that finds its way onto my lips.

Last night I sent my final text to Ethan, officially letting him go. I couldn't stick around and wait any longer for him to show up and come through. I knew he'd let me go, too, but it was hard to believe he would give up so easily after everything we've been through.

I thought he was my future. When we started dating, it was something fun. I was extremely attracted to him and we had a connection, and no, I'm not bullshitting. We really did connect, and being with him was easy aside from all the ex-fiancée bull.

That was really what made me the craziest, and I wonder if it would have been different if none of that drama had happened. Would he be getting on the plane with me tomorrow?

Originally, I wasn't supposed to come help on this trip. I didn't want to take away from packing time, but the idea of getting away from Acton was too good to pass up. Being there was miserable.

We pull up to the service entrance of the fancy building and are greeted by the event coordinator, who's not glammed out like I'd thought she'd be after I talked to her on the phone to assure her everything would be fine.

On the phone, she sounded a little paranoid that the event was going to be a disaster or something and I guess I judged her based off that, but now I feel bad.

She is wearing a t-shirt with cutoffs and flip-flops; her hair is bright red, and she is gorgeous. I feel frumpy wearing my black pants and apron.

"Hi! I'm Melissa! It's so nice to finally meet you in person!" She shakes both my mom's hand and mine excitedly like she can't believe we're here.

"You too! You want to tell us where to set up?" My mom takes the lead like the genius she is, and we head into the building.

Inside, it's a completely different environment. It's dark, but there are white and blue lights that make it feel like we're under water, and now I understand the color of the cupcakes that was requested.

In the middle is a dance floor, and various people are setting the tables with wine and water glasses. Giant centerpieces sit in the middle of each one, and it looks like a million-dollar wedding in here.

The cupcake display is ginormous and stacked high; I'm looking at it wondering how the hell we're supposed to get cupcakes up to the top and how people are supposed to get them down.

"Okay, I see your look there," Melissa says, and I quickly school my features as she chuckles. "It's okay. So, basically because you're also helping us serve them, we have a step ladder that will be in the back. Around nine o'clock, we'll start serving the cupcakes, which is why the display is so big. It's art until dessert, and eventually we'll put all the cupcakes on plates and pass them out."

She moves around the display as she talks, and my mom takes in every word while I hang back. I know I should be invested in this, but my heart isn't in it today.

When they're finally done chatting, Mom and I head back and start wheeling boxes of cupcakes into the building. While I trek back and forth, Mom starts stacking them on the display. The cupcakes are still cold, which is great, because they're going to be on display for about four hours.

When the last cupcake is placed, Mom and I leave to have dinner before we're stuck behind a table for the rest of the night.

Walking downtown is kind of fun. There are different types of people on every corner, and the buildings tower over me and go on forever.

From a distance, Denver looks so small. When you're

driving on the highway, it's tiny, but when you get into the heart of the city, it's like another world.

We find a Mexican food place that makes giant burritos and decide to give it a try. When we're seated at our table with our food, my mom starts prying. Gotta give it to her, she waited a long time.

"Okay, so I have to know what happened." She picks through her food with a fork then glances up at me.

"What happened with what?" I ask, avoiding it because it hurts.

"With Ethan, honey. You guys were starting something great then out of nowhere you're over?"

I sigh and take a bite of my burrito. I'm sad, not dead, and this food is delicious. After I swallow, I look up and tell her, "There's not much to tell, Mom."

"Well, try anyway."

I look around the restaurant, stalling for a minute. "I got this note at the bakery from his ex, and it was threatening. It's not the first time she's tried to get between us, but this time I lost it. I went to Ethan and asked him to make her stop. Then he stopped talking to me. He ignored my calls and texts." I sigh again.

She crinkles her forehead in confusion. "That makes no sense. He was so in love with you."

My eyes start to feel hot and watery, and I blink before tears can escape. "I loved him too, but he doesn't want to be with me anymore."

"I just find that very hard to believe."

"I don't want to talk about it anymore."

Mom nods her head in understanding. "Okay, well, let's talk about something that makes me sad—you are leaving tomorrow! I can't believe it."

I smile. My only true relief from the personal hell I'm in is the fact that I start my trip tomorrow. I decided with everything going on, I'd move it up a week and start the next chapter of my life.

I thought maybe after I texted Ethan goodbye last night he might try to change my mind, fight for me, or *something*, but nothing happened, not even a simple acknowledgment text back. It broke off the final piece of my heart and made me leap into action, immediately changing my ticket to the soonest out-of-country flight.

"I'm excited to start my trip." I smile at Mom and continue eating, pushing Ethan out of my thoughts once again.

"I actually thought your brother was going to cry." Mom giggles a little, imagining my brother's eyes tearing up. It was a sweet moment.

"I know. I've got to remember to call Kate tomorrow before I leave. I'd feel bad not telling her I left."

Mom waves me off. "She'll be all right, and she'll be here soon enough." She gestures to our surroundings.

"True." Kate will love living in Denver; it suits her personality perfectly. She's always been outgoing, and this city is perfect for that kind of person.

We finish our food and throw our trash away then head back toward the event center. I'm looking forward to the evening being over and done and leaving tomorrow.

The event starts, and I immediately wish I'd worn something nicer than this, because everyone here is dressed to the nines. It must be some charity, but I wasn't paying enough attention to who the coordinator worked for to remember.

We stand around waiting for the everyone to start eating. People are being seated and a speaker gets up to start the speeches—I guess that's the catch: you have to suffer through speeches before you can eat.

Bored, I pull my phone out and start texting Kate, letting her know about my departure in the morning, hoping she won't be pissed. She doesn't answer the text, but I'm not surprised.

I'm scrolling through my Instagram page, aimlessly liking photo after photo, ready to go to bed when I feel eyes on me. Peeking up from my phone, my eyes scan the immediate area, not noticing anyone, and I think maybe I've finally lost my damn mind.

Just then, someone approaches the table. I look up at him and freeze, my heart stopping in my chest. I'm staring into the eyes of Stormy Guy and wondering why he's here, of all places.

"Aveline," he says, his voice smooth. He's dressed in a fancy tux just like the rest of the men at the event, his hair is styled perfectly, and he looks like a GQ model, but his demeanor still freaks me out.

"Um, hi." I look around and see my mom ten feet to my right, talking to Melissa. "What's your name again?" I didn't ask before, and he didn't feel compelled to tell me.

"David." He reaches a hand out for mine and I reciprocate. "How have you been?"

I chuckle nervously, trying to appear relaxed. "Uh, fine. I'm sorry, how do you know me?"

He smiles and resembles a Greek god. If he weren't so creepy, I'd probably find him sexy. "Mutual friends."

I cock my head. "Oh yeah? Who's that?"

"Ethan Hart."

My brows scrunch together. This guy is friends with Ethan? "And how is it that you know Ethan?"

He relaxes his stance, but it looks like he's forcing himself. "We served in the military together."

I think hard about who Ethan has told me about. He told me his tragic story with the bomb, and I remember that Brad was the guy who passed in the accident. David was his best friend.

David hates Ethan, so why is he here?

"Uh, excuse me just a minute."

I rush to my mom and tell her I'm running to the bathroom. When I locate it, I run into a stall and unlock my phone. I pull up Ethan's contact and try to calm my breathing as it rings.

When it goes to voicemail, I growl in frustration. Why won't he just answer his damn phone? "Ethan, it's me. Look, I know you hate me for whatever reason, but you have to help me. Your ex-Marine buddy David—he's here. I don't think he has good intentions and he's freaking me out. Please call me back."

I hang up the phone and close my eyes, trying to breathe. I don't know what David wants, but I know it's not good. Why would he be here?

I call Ethan again and get his voicemail. I don't leave another message, knowing now that he won't answer me.

Braving leaving the safety of the bathroom, I push the door open and peer around. I can't see much from here, but I step out and head toward the cupcake display—only I don't make it, because everything goes black.

# CHAPTER THIRTY-TWO

*Ethan*
*12 hours earlier*

I FIND DAVID. I searched all night, went to every single hotel and motel within fifty miles, which took a lot longer than I expected. By the time I make it back to Acton, all I want to do is find my pillow and sleep. Exhaustion threatens to overcome me, but I made a promise, and my next stop is the bakery to see if Aveline is there. It's time to come clean with her.

Pulling my phone out, I open Walters' contact and tap the icon to call him.

"Walters."

"Hey, do you have anything new for me?"

"Sorry, man. Nothing new. He withdrew a thousand

bucks from his account that last time, and I'm sure it's getting him by pretty well."

I sigh and rub my aching eyes. Nothing is going my way with this stupid fucking game he's playing. He didn't reply to my email, which pissed me off even more.

I hang up with Walters after being reassured that he's going to let me know whenever something happens. Hopefully, that will happen soon.

I park my truck in front of the bakery and walk inside. It's busy, which makes sense at eight in the morning, and Kate is rushing around, looking more frazzled than usual. I wait my turn in line, knowing my privileges of sneaking around with Aveline in the back of the bakery are long gone.

When I step up to the counter, Kate asks what I need without looking at me. When she finally sees that it's me, she glares. "You look like shit." She crosses her arms and holds her stance firm.

"I bet. Look, can you tell Aveline I'm here? It's really important."

She scoffs at me and her eyes radiate disbelief. "You're out of your mind. I wouldn't be a good friend if I allowed you to keep hurting her, and that's all you're doing now—hurting her."

My heart clenches, knowing Aveline has shared her sadness and pain with her friend. "Look, I know I've been a shitty boyfriend, all right?" Boyfriend feels inadequate for what I feel for this girl. "But you have to know I've been doing this for her safety. I need to tell her what's going on."

Kate stares at me for a minute. "Shitty boyfriend is an understatement." She sighs. "Ethan, I can't be the bodyguard here and you're holding up the line, so I'll tell you one thing: she's not here."

I rub my head, confused. She almost always works on Saturdays. "Where is she?" Kate shakes her head and motions for me to move. I slap my hand down. "Please, Kate, tell me where she is!" I'm desperate and it comes through in my voice. I've never felt so needy in my life.

The resolve disappears from Kate's eyes. "She's in Denver, helping out with the big event. She'll be back Monday."

I walk away immediately. Monday is too far away; she needs to know now. I contemplate calling her but know how shitty it would be to call her after all this time. Plus, who knows if she would even answer the phone.

The only way I can tell her and not have her hate me is talking face to face. Then I can also protect her from David.

Deciding sleep is the only way I'll make it to Denver, I head home, shower, and pass out. My dreams are of Aveline, just as they should be—her laughing, her loving eyes looking into mine when I tell her she's mine forever—and it's the best rest I've had in weeks.

Then the nightmare takes hold. We're back to the Cliffs of Moher, and this time, we both fall, unable to protect each other.

I wake with a start and throw shit in a bag before jumping into my truck and peeling out of my driveway. I'm ending this nightmare today.

My charger isn't working. It will charge for two seconds then stop, and I growl in frustration. I know she's in Denver, but have no clue where. I need to call her and find her, but I can't if I don't have a phone that works.

I've been driving for two hours and am finally starting to see the Denver skyline. My dream has made me a nervous wreck, but right now I'm not sure if reality and dream world are colliding, and that's what sets my nerves on edge.

I kick myself again when I think that I could have charged my phone at home and then wouldn't be fighting with the battery life right now, something I maybe would have remembered if I'd had any real sleep the last few weeks.

Moving the cord slightly, it starts to work, and I hold my breath. Holding the steering wheel with my other hand, I send up a quick prayer, hoping it will hold a charge.

The city is lit up brightly, and it's beautiful if I take the time to look at it as I pull into the Saturday night traffic. It's busy with everyone in a hurry to get to whatever event or bar they're searching for, and groups of people walk around, laughing and talking without a care.

I search for somewhere to park, not knowing where I'm going to be heading just yet. Once parked, I look at my phone and curse when I see the screen is still black.

The night grows darker around me and I sigh. This whole mess has me stressed and shaking my head at how ridiculous my life has been. I can't believe this is what it has come to—our innocent relationship turned into a bargaining chip with a crazy person hell-bent on getting revenge.

I check the clock on my dashboard: it's nine thirty now, and I have no clue where Aveline is hidden away in this giant city. I don't know where she was working or where she would choose to stay.

Waiting twenty more minutes, I pick my phone up and sigh with relief that the screen finally lights up with power.

It's barely on for a second when two missed calls and voicemail from Aveline show on the screen. My heart starts beating faster, but before I can see what she said, another call comes in from a number I don't recognize.

I answer with hesitation, "Hello."

"Ethan?" The voice on the other end sounds like an older Aveline.

"Belle?"

"Oh, Ethan! I'm sorry to bother you, but have you heard from Aveline by chance?"

My eyebrows scrunch, confused. "I have a voicemail from her—what's wrong?"

"She's not here. She went to the restroom but she never came back, and now she's not answering her phone."

Belle sounds panicked, the worry in her voice making it clear that something has happened to her daughter.

"Okay, let me call you right back." We hang up and I take a deep breath before I tap to play the voicemail. My stomach is in knots, my palms are sweaty, and my heart is pounding.

My hand shakes when I lift the phone and listen as Aveline's voice fills my ear.

"Ethan, it's me. Look, I know you hate me for whatever reason, but you have to help me. Your ex-Marine buddy David—he's here. I don't think he has good intentions and he's freaking me out. Please call me back."

"Fuck!" I slam my hand against the steering wheel and groan. Quickly, I redial Belle and find out where she is then throw my truck in gear and peel out of the parking lot.

The entire way over, I think about what David's plan is, what game he thinks he could possibly be playing and how he thinks he'll come out of this unscathed after kidnapping an innocent woman—not only that, kidnapping *my* innocent woman.

If I have anything to do with it, he'll be lucky to come out of this alive.

The event they were working at is by Coors Field and I park close by. By the time I show up to the building, I have a hard time finding any spots because there are police cars everywhere.

Finally finding one, I jump out and run as fast as my knee allows me. The place is swarmed with well-dressed people, attendees of the event I assume, and police are spread out questioning people.

"Sorry, sir, you're not permitted in this area." A uniformed officer holds his hand up to me and I remind myself that I can't injure him.

"I'm looking for MaeBelle Montgomery—she called and told me my girlfriend is missing. I also have evidence for your officers. I know who took her."

The officer looks at me, trying to gauge if I'm telling the truth or not, and he must decide I am because he motions with his head for me to follow him.

We move through the crowd and toward a police car where I see Belle being questioned by another officer.

When she sees me, she leaves the officer without another word and throws her arms around me, I don't know what's happened or what they know about Aveline, but I cling to her, hoping I can offer her some sort of support without falling apart myself.

"Ethan." She sighs, looking into my eyes, the worry on her face evident. "My baby is gone, Ethan."

"Gone?" My heart starts racing, the word repeating itself over and over. "What do you mean she's gone?"

"The police have no leads yet. They've questioned so many people and no one saw her. Where did she go?"

Breathing air into my tight lungs, I try to gather the words I need to tell the woman who welcomed me into her family that this is all my fault. "Belle, we need an officer. I know who took her."

Her eyes widen at the words 'took her', but like the understanding person she is, she nods her head and flags down the officer she was talking to before she spotted me.

We go to a more secluded area, the chief of police comes over to talk to us, and I explain who David is and what he's been threatening. Then, with a hand over my heart, I let them listen to the voicemail Aveline left—the message she left because I missed her call due to a faulty charger.

With the new information, the officers start scurrying around, some jumping in their cruisers and taking off.

"We need you both to come down to the station. You'll wait there until we find out more, and we may need to ask more questions." The chief is Mathew Himmel. He's an aging man, something I imagine has happened over the years in a stressful profession. He's fit though, and he looks straight at you when he's speaking as a sign of respect, something I myself was taught in the military.

We get into my truck, Belle being unable to drive a vehicle right now, and follow his cruiser to the police station.

She reaches over and grasps my hand, and I don't even hesitate gripping hers back. We sit in the deafening silence, both of us understanding the seriousness of the situation, hoping, praying the outcome we fear won't become a reality.

"I have to call Lucas," Belle whispers, not to initiate a discussion with me but just needing to voice out loud the thought that she needs to tell her son his sister was kidnapped.

Pulling up to the station, we find a place to park the truck, and once it's in place, I hang my head, the first tears ready to escape. "I'm so sorry, Mrs. Montgomery."

I don't explain what I'm apologizing for; the list feels far too long to get into, and I know after we know for sure what's happened, Belle will hate me almost as much as I hate myself.

"Ethan." Her firm voice makes me suck up my tears and look up to take whatever she needs to dole out. "You look at me."

I look into her eyes and there's worry there, but also a strong determination, like whatever she's about to say is something she needs me to understand.

"You did not make this our reality." I open my mouth to argue and she holds up her hand, silencing me. "You didn't. I know you feel responsible, and I know you are hurting like I am, but this is all on *him*. Every single thing that has happened, every feeling you are feeling—it is all his fault. Do you understand?"

I nod, the first tear spilling over. I don't even have it in me to feel embarrassed by it.

"Aveline is such a strong girl, and I believe—I have to believe she will make it through this. We have to hold on to that hope. Do not give up."

She pulls me toward her and we meet in the middle, her crushing me in a hug only a mom can give, and I let go. Then I cry. I cry because I'm hurt, I cry because I'm fucking scared, I cry because the girl I love is in a position she never would have been in had it not been for me.

Then, I stop and look at Belle. She nods, giving me a

stern look. "Good. Now, let's find our girl."

# CHAPTER THIRTY-THREE

*Aveline*

MY HEAD IS pounding, I swear I'm seeing stars, and I don't want to pry my eyes open. I groan but stop before I get too loud, realizing I have no idea where I am. I'm confined somewhere. I feel movement, and for some weird reason, I feel like I'm in a boat.

I know that's not possible though—why would I be in a boat?

I can't remember why I'm here or how I got to this place, but I try to think back to what I was doing before. The questions that pop into my head are the ones you'd hear a doctor ask a patient who's been in a coma.

*Do you know your name?*
*How old are you?*

*What year is it?*
*What did you eat for breakfast?*
The last one may have had a bit of a creative license, but still. The thing is, I wouldn't know if the answers were correct since no one is here to corroborate them.

*Ugh.* I grab my head as a sharp pain shoots through the back of it. My hair is sticky with something and I pull my hand in front of my face, but I can't even see what's on it because it's too dark.

Finally, I look at my surroundings: I'm lying on my back, and I'm still moving. I conclude that I'm in the back of a trunk when I notice the faint red glow from the brake lights.

It stinks so bad back here, like a gym bag you leave in your car for like a year. *Oh, you've never done that? Yeah, no, me either.*

I search my pockets and sigh when I don't find my phone anywhere. Obviously if someone took me, they'd probably be smart enough to take my phone.

I still myself and close my eyes, willing my brain to think harder at figuring out what the hell happened, and then it hits me all at once.

I was working the big event in Denver with Mom, and we were about to serve the cupcakes off that ridiculous display when I had to go to the bathroom. *Right?*

I search my brain, visualizing the events like rewinding a DVR. Then I remember something else: David was there—David who I had no idea who he was, David who said he was friends with Ethan.

But that was a lie—they aren't friends. He hates Ethan...*right?*

My brain is so foggy I nearly cry just trying to remember. I went to the bathroom and called Ethan, I think...but when I came out, that's where it all ends. That's all I remember, and now I'm here.

A tear leaks out and I silently scold myself, knowing I need to knock if off. Crying won't help me.

Hopefully, someone saw David grab me. How can you sneak out of a giant building where a huge event is going on with an unconscious person in tow and no one notice? The hope rises in my chest. Someone definitely saw—I have to believe that.

I have to.

I think about my mom, who is probably freaking out because I never came back. I wonder how long ago that was. I feel like I slept a while, but there's no way to tell what time it is.

I think about Ethan, who maybe got my voicemail, but maybe he ignored it. It's not like we were on good terms or anything. He probably thought I was trying to be bitchy again. I immediately regret how we've spoken to each other, praying those aren't the last things I get to say to him.

I know he is a good guy; really deep down, that's what I know. He does care about me, and he cares about the people in his life. I just wish we could have made it work.

I still love him, and I still want him, despite how the last month or so has gone. I've played it off in front of everyone, trying to not allow them to see how affected I am by the entire thing, but I am so hurt.

I thought he and I were going to make it. Not every person would be willing to go on a trip with someone they'd known that short of a time, or even be willing to wait until I got home.

He did love me at some point, and I just hope deep

down he still does and listens to that damn voicemail.

Deep in my thoughts, I barely even notice that we've slowed down until the car comes to a complete stop. My breath picks up and I try to calm myself, doing anything I can to breathe normally.

I hear a key scratch on something and I close my eyes, pretending to still be knocked out. The trunk door opens—no surprise he stuffed me in a trunk, crazy jerk—and a bright light almost forces my eyes open, but I hold strong.

*Don't move a muscle*, I tell myself. David doesn't say anything and doesn't touch me; it seems like he is making sure I'm not doing anything against the rules.

*The rules of being kidnapped—huh, I wonder if they sell that handbook. I could use it right about now.*

He starts to close the door and I risk opening my eyes, hoping I can see where we are. It's still dark out but that doesn't tell me what time it is. I do know we're parked at a gas station somewhere because I saw a pump and the brightness was the florescent lights all gas stations use.

When the door is fully shut, I start to catch my breath. I wish I knew what his plan is, how far we are going—anything. Is he going to shoot me or hold me against my will to get back at Ethan?

Not knowing what I'm going to do, my eyes drift shut when the car starts moving again, moving farther away from my family, from my life, and from Ethan.

Unable to help it, I fall asleep in that trunk, hoping when I wake up, it'll just have been a terrible nightmare.

I wake up in the same position, in the same car, in the same damn trunk I fell asleep in. *Damn.*

Sleeping away reality didn't work.

The car is still in motion, but this time I see through the cracks that the sun is shining through, so I know it's the next day. We've driven all night long—who knows where we are by now.

I know I'm stuck with a psycho, and I know nothing good will come of this horrible dream I'm living, but I can't help but wonder if they're looking for me. My mother has to be going out of her mind. Did she call the cops? Are they even trying? Are they on their way?

The car, I realize, is a piece of crap. I haven't the slightest idea what model it is, but I can tell it's a few decades old.

I try to think of anything positive about my situation. Even though I want to just wallow in a pessimistic place for a while, it won't help anything.

What's good if I die? Well, they can use my trip fund to cover the funeral expenses, so that's good. I'd hate to leave a debt for my family.

Another positive is I'll never have to see Ethan and Marie together, even though it's also a negative because I'll never see Ethan again.

*Okay, wait—positive thoughts.*

I'll get to see my dad again, and that's something I can smile about. I miss him. He was my hero and seeing him wouldn't be so bad, but then I'd be leaving Mom and Lucas alone.

Sighing, I shake all those thoughts from my head. This is definitely not helping like I thought it might.

What kind of things do people in the movies do when they get shoved into a trunk? Surely I've seen a dozen or so where this has happened, and I must have learned something.

I feel around the small trunk, twisting to my other side, trying to relieve the cramp my left cheek is starting to feel. My hand runs over everything on the top, looking for a lever or some sort of latch to undo the trunk.

I can barely see in here, but I do see sun through the taillights and the cracks in the trunk door. I release a breath and drop my hands.

Then, a light bulb, and because I think I'm losing it, I swear one literally pops up above my head.

Reaching to touch around the brake light, I feel something give way and realize this light is already partially broken. I push as hard as I can, and a piece of it pops off. I pray he doesn't see it in the rearview mirror and wait with bated breath to see if he stops.

I reach around in the trunk for something to stick out of the light to signal that someone is in here. I hope someone is behind us; from this angle, I can't see any cars, but I do hear some traffic.

Not finding anything to stick out, I take a deep breath and will myself to calm down. The last resort has become my only option, and I roll my eyes at my prudishness.

Unclasping my bra, I wiggle around like a circus acrobat to get it off in the small space. I have a hard enough time when I'm not stuck in a trunk.

I turn myself so I can see where I'm sticking this thing. Finding the small hole, I start pushing the bra through and almost let go of the strap when the wind catches it.

Then, I wait and hope a smart stranger will see it before David does.

# CHAPTER THIRTY-FOUR

*Ethan*

THE MOOD IN the hotel room is somber. Everyone is silent, lost in his or her own mind with the tragedy we all feel deeply.

*Too bad I quit smoking—I could use one right about now.*

Sometime in the middle of the night, Lucas and his grandparents showed up at the police station. It was the signal that the chief needed to send us someplace to wait things out.

They hadn't had any luck in tracking David down when we left, and every second that ticked by was like another nail in Aveline's coffin. I didn't want to think she was already dead, really, but in the back of my mind, I didn't see any reason for him to take her away and not find someplace to dump her body.

If that was the case, my life as I knew it was over.

The future we were planning, the house we wanted, the bakery she was going to run, the kids I wanted to have with her—all those dreams we'd dreamed together were gone.

Lucas sighs and sits next to me on the bed. He hasn't said much the entire time he's been here, but I know he's feeling the hurt as much as I am.

"Can I ask you something?" His question startles me out of my daze.

I clear my throat, not having spoken yet today. "Yeah, bud."

He hesitates like he's afraid to ask the question on his mind. "Did you really break up with Aveline for Marie?"

I furrow my brow, not at all having expected him to say that. "What the hell are you talking about?"

He shrugs, keeping his gaze on the TV. "You and Aveline kind of broke it off unexpectedly and then she told me you were with Marie, which I didn't see coming. I didn't even really believe it until Marie confirmed the rumor right to Aveline's face."

My blood boils. Of course Marie would capitalize on the situation, something I didn't even think about.

"No, that's not at all what happened."

He turns to me then, his eyes full of sadness and defeat. "What happened then?"

I decide now is the time to come clean with the family. Belle has been half listening to us anyway—it's not like we're in a penthouse. The room is small, and you can hear every creak in the place.

Starting with the emails, I explain who David is to me,

some of which Belle knows from hearing me explain it to the cops. I tell them about the pictures that were texted to Aveline, the notes we both received, and then finally him talking to her and Kate outside the bar.

I push through the terrible memories and tell them about the mission in Afghanistan when everything went to hell. I tell them about Brad and his death, how I was supposed to be the one in charge and how his death was all my fault. I explain that that's what David can't get over, what he can't move on from.

They all stay silent as I explain the anguish I've experienced and put others through. Their eyes stay unchanged, no judgment there, only sympathy showing on their faces.

I tell them about how I pushed her away, even though it was the last thing I really wanted, to try to take her away as a target for him. I tell them how I didn't tell her what was going on because I knew she'd refuse to let me handle it, and this is when Belle cracks her first smile, thinking about her stubborn daughter, no doubt.

When I'm done, I feel like a weight has been lifted off my chest. Now it is completely up to them whether they forgive me or not.

"You did good, son." This comes from Aveline's grandpa. He looks sad but doesn't seem upset about what I've told them, just about the situation in general.

"I know now it probably wasn't the best choice, but I wanted to protect her. That was the job I wanted." Admitting that feels shameful, but it's true. I want to be Aveline's protector, which makes this hurt even more, knowing I've failed.

"That's the job she wants you to have." Belle sits at the end of the bed and looks at me. "She loves you. You both are so young and have so much to look forward to. It will all work out."

I hang my head, ashamed that I've felt so defeated over the last twenty-four hours and Aveline's mom has taken on the job of positive thinker, praying and hoping for our girl to be alive and believing it.

"Wait! Turn that up!" Grandma jumps up from the bed she's on and we crank the TV. The news is covering a high-speed chase down Interstate 25. The car immediately looks familiar and I curse, ignoring everyone in the room, my eyes glued to the screen.

The car is going way too fast, and something is hanging out the back. The helicopter has a little trouble keeping up with the cars, the camera zooming in and out, trying to focus. Several cop cars are in pursuit of the vehicle, and you can see all the other cars off to the side or trying to swerve out of the way.

We're silent again, trying to hear the news anchor explain what is going on.

"Police are in pursuit of a David Maller. He is believed to be in possession of a 21-year-old woman named Aveline Montgomery. Police have been looking for her since last night when she disappeared from an event in Denver, Colorado, that she was catering with her mother. Civilians in New Mexico called in to report a strange piece of clothing hanging through the brake light of the car, and police were immediately dispatched to the location.

"Other information from the Denver Police Department confirms that David was attempting revenge on Ms. Montgomery's boyfriend, Ethan Hart, a former Marine who was involved in an IED explosion in Afghanistan at the beginning of last year that left Maller's best friend, Brad

Langford, dead.

"We will continue to watch this as it unfolds and update everyone as more information comes in."

The TV stays on the chase, the anchors talking over the video, trying to explain the situation to people as they watch.

I'm up and out the door, not waiting for anyone to follow and running out toward my truck. Of course, everyone follows and asks me what I'm doing.

"She's like nine hours away, maybe more!" I yell and then breathe, trying to control the anger I feel building in my chest. "I'm going to be there as soon as I can. She'll need us."

They look at me then at each other. They head back in and grab their things before all filing out of the room. Belle and her parents get into their car while Lucas climbs into the passenger seat of mine. He nods at me, on board with whatever I need to do. Maybe they feel the same way and were just scared to show it.

Thinking about Aveline in that car, being tossed around in the trunk, scared out of her mind makes me crazy, and I can't wait to get my hands on that fucker.

I look at the other car and then get into my truck, cranking the engine and tearing out of the parking lot, ready to see Aveline, ready to kill David.

# CHAPTER THIRTY-FIVE

*Aveline*

*WELL, THAT WAS a terrible idea.*

My stomach rolls again as the car's speed increases and it moves from side to side. Sirens blare behind us and I'm about to puke that burrito I had last night all over the place.

I don't know if it's dehydration, lack of vision, or the swerving that's making me sick, or maybe it's all three.

As it turns out, someone saw my bra and did exactly what I needed: they called the cops. However, instead of pulling over like I thought he would, David sped up—a lot. He's going much faster than I thought this car could even go and it is probably very dangerous, but I can't think about that.

So, I'm pretty sure I am in the middle of a full-fledged police chase, which is kind of exciting to watch but not as fun to be in.

My stomach clenches and I can't hold it in anymore. Rolling to the side as much as I can, I puke all over the trunk. I'm partially lying in it, and I pray to God this will end soon because more bile is already starting to rise.

My mind, being the one that it is, starts to wonder if this is being televised, and part of me hopes not because then everyone is going to see my bra...*right, not important right now.*

The other part of me is curious to see what it would look like, and if a news station is watching this then I can watch it later myself—that is, if I live to see daylight again.

"Pull over immediately!" The voice booms from one of the police cars and I startle, not expecting that. Instead of listening like he should, the vehicle lurches forward again.

The police officer repeats himself and then the voice is muffled again. I lose my vision and think I'm about to pass out or puke again, I can't be sure which.

The car swerves again and a horn blares, I'm sure from another car trying to get out of the way of the madman on the loose.

Suddenly, something hits the back part of the car, jostling me around. Everything jerks to the side and if I'm correct, David overcorrects and hits something.

It doesn't stop the car, though; instead it pushes us up and suddenly gravity takes over. My body is slung from side to side, up and down. My head hits the hard metal more times than I can count and then sunlight streams into my face.

My eyes widen when I see the ground coming for my face, and I pull my arms and legs in as best as I can in the hope that I can save myself from too many broken bones.

I hit the ground and slide. My vision is partially obscured but I see it before it happens: the car comes toward me, still flying through the air.

I stare at it, wondering if after all that, this is the end.

Before it lands, my vision gives in to the darkness, and suddenly there's nothing.

## ETHAN

THE HOSPITAL SMELL grates on my nerves the longer I have to wait. Waiting is all we've done.

As it turns out, they were only seven hours away, and the conclusion is that they must have pulled off somewhere between Denver and here.

We're in Albuquerque, New Mexico, at University Hospital, the closest one at the time of the accident. The police had him cornered, but one of the officers decided to nudge the back end of the car where Aveline was and it made David panic, so he overcorrected and hit the median with the piece-of-shit car.

The trunk opened during a flip and Aveline got thrown, and not only that, the car also landed on her.

Now, we're waiting, and I don't know her status, don't know if she's responsive—I don't know *anything*, and it's pissing me off.

The only reason we know what happened was because the officers on the scene came to the hospital to try to get a statement from her. Belle intercepted them and got the story, each of us growing angrier and angrier the more details he shared.

I get the urge to find David. I know he's here and I know he must be banged up, but I want to make him hurt. I want to make him suffer—he deserves it.

He took what was mine, he hurt her, and he was planning to do more damage. My inner devil wants him dead.

We sit there forever; the night has darkened the sky

outside, and I try to remember how long this has all been going on.

Did I only drive to Denver just last night? Has it really only been twenty-four hours since this nightmare became reality?

Belle sighs and announces she needs coffee. Her parents go with her and promise to bring some back. Lucas has gone back to being the silent man; we haven't had much to talk about anyway, not without knowing what Aveline's status is.

As far as we know, she's alive, and that's more than I could have hoped for. I don't care how long her recovery takes; I'll stay with her, I'll help her, I'll do anything and everything she needs.

I'm never leaving her side again.

Lucas moves and reaches his hand into his pocket, pulling his phone out. He looks at the screen and unlocks it to answer a call.

"Hey." He listens to the person on other end. "Yeah, we're here." Pause. "You are?" He looks up suddenly and stands. "No, wait there. I'll come to you."

I frown. "Who's that?"

He puts his phone away. "Kate. She's here. I'm going to go get her."

I watch as he leaves the waiting room. I didn't even think about Kate this whole time even though I know they have grown close. I should've thought about her when everything was going down, but all I could focus on was if Aveline was alive or not.

I sigh and rub my hands over my head. I'm starting to think I can't wait any longer when someone finally emerges from the room we weren't permitted to enter. Just as I stand, Belle comes back holding two coffees. She sees me and I motion to the doctor right as he calls Aveline's name.

We quickly walk over to him, all eager and uncertain about how we'll feel after he gives us an update.

"Thank you for being patient, I know you've been waiting a while."

"How's my daughter?" Belle drills him with a look that tells him to not beat around the bush.

"She's doing all right." A collective sigh comes out of our mouths, and I notice Lucas and Kate join the group. Kate puts a hand on my shoulder, and it's a surprising comfort.

The doctor clears his throat. "She's got bumps and bruises on 90% of her body, and she has three broken ribs, which we've wrapped. She broke her right arm, we're guessing when she finally made impact with the ground.

"We've done tests and scans and there are no signs of internal bleeding, which is a huge blessing. She's still unconscious. She gained consciousness when she first arrived, but we've kept her heavily sedated, trying to allow her body to heal."

"Thank Jesus," says Aveline's grandma, bowing her head.

"Can we see her?" Belle asks.

"Of course, but only two at a time, and just family." He waits for the decision, and I take a step back. As much as I want to see her, the last thing I deserve is to be the first one to see her after everything I've done.

"I'll take Ethan, then you guys can go." My head shoots up; I'm surprised Belle is choosing me first. She grabs my hand and doesn't ask, just pulls me along. The doctor looks at her and she says, "He's her fiancé." He nods and walks through the doors.

We follow the doctor and I struggle to keep my head up.

I feel like my heart is going to pound out of my chest. I'm about to see Aveline at her worst, literally her worst, and it's all on me.

We walk down the brightly lit hall, all blinking florescent lights. I know I'll never forget this moment, walking down this hall to see her, taking in the smells and the sounds. Everything is overwhelming, and all I want to do is leave.

We come up to the door in the ICU where all the rooms are in a circle. Every one looks occupied, but I can't see the patients, just the lights and the nurses coming and going. The doctor stands to the side and gestures for us to enter her room; he stays outside.

Belle lets go of my hand and without her pulling me, I stay rooted in place, knowing after I look behind the curtain, I won't be able to forgive myself.

Belle gasps, her hands go to her mouth, and tears fall down her cheeks. She starts sobbing, slowly moving toward the head of the bed, and I suddenly can't wait any longer. I move forward, bracing myself.

I'm not one to be dramatic, but the second I see her face, I lose my breath. I can't breathe, and tears come so fast I don't even register that I'm crying.

I turn away and press my forehead to the wall behind me, trying to get my bearings. I feel a hand press into my shoulder.

"She's okay, Ethan. Our girl is okay." Belle sounds like she's still crying, but she pulls me around and pushes me toward the bed.

Aveline looks peaceful under all the bruising, but unfortunately, there is bruising everywhere. She has a bandage on her face that I'm guessing is covering a cut, and another one is wrapped around her head. I don't know what happened there.

I want to wash her of all the pain, all the bruising, all the cuts and inevitable scars. I want to rewind the last week, the last month. I want to take her home, to my home, and ravish her in our bed, want to wake up to her cooking us breakfast, want to watch her read on the porch while I work.

I want to fix everything I've broken.

Grabbing her hand, I gently bring it to my lips. Taking the chair next to the bed, I watch her. She only has an oxygen tube, and the rest of her looks normal—other than the giant cast on her right arm, that is, but that will heal.

"I'm so sorry, baby." My voice cracks and I breathe through my nose. I shake my head. "I'm sorry I put you through all of this. I promise I'll never hurt you again if you'll forgive me. God…" I pull in a shaky breath. "Please forgive me, Aveline."

I stare at her face, wondering what I was thinking with pushing her away. I wish I could go back in time and kick my own ass.

Belle stands behind me and places her hands on my shoulders. We stay silent, probably both hoping she'll magically wake up and be her normal joyful self.

"She's going to need some help, and you know how disappointed she'll be to miss her trip, but we can't let her down now."

I nod, agreeing with her. "I'm not going anywhere."

She grips my shoulder. "Thatta boy."

We stay for another twenty minutes before we head back to the waiting room to allow her grandparents to go back, and after that, Kate and Lucas go back. Her grandparents return with red eyes and I can't help but hug them both, trying to comfort them the way they've comforted me.

I call a nearby hotel and book a couple of rooms for everyone. No one is ready to head back to Acton just yet, and we all need rest between visits. Once that's set, I offer to take the grandparents to the hotel and get them settled—anything I can do to help after screwing up so bad.

When they're settled, I head to the other room and shower, trying to feel normal and not allow guilt to flood me too much. Keeping my eyes on the prize, I order room service for the grandparents and stop to get everyone else some food on the way back.

I get back to the hospital and only find Kate in the waiting room, looking at her phone. She seems to be immersed and doesn't look up when I sit down.

"Hey," I say, handing her a burger.

She smiles gratefully and takes it before returning to her phone. She turns the screen toward me and I see it's a picture of all of us at the campsite last month. We look so freaking happy.

"She was so happy with you."

The bite I just took turns cold in my mouth and I force it down my throat. "She will be again."

"I believe you." Setting her phone down, she unwraps her burger. "Lucas told me everything, and I'm sorry you went through all of that."

I shake my head. "It's my own fault."

"No, it's not."

I don't argue; it's pointless with her and with Belle. I don't know how everyone else feels, but it seems like I'm not going to win this particular argument with them.

We sit and talk about the fun summer we had, and I

think about how I get along with Kate better than I ever thought I would. Belle and Lucas emerge, and when I give them their food, they give me grateful smiles. They seem lighter now that we know Aveline is going to be okay.

    I head back to her room and take my seat, and then I wait for her to wake up, praying she'll forgive me when she does.

# CHAPTER THIRTY-SIX

*Aveline*

MY HEAD IS pounding, and I'm pretty sure that means I'm not dead. God wouldn't torture me with headaches in heaven, I'm sure of that. Pinching my eyes, I try opening them one at a time, trying to figure out where I am.

Am I still locked in a trunk? Where's David?

Then I remember—*oh yeah, I got Hulk-smashed by a car. How in the hell am I still alive?*

I open my eyes and am assaulted by bright lights. "Ugh!" I raise my right arm to cover my eyes, but it doesn't actually come. *Oh God, did I lose my arm?* I look down, trying to shift, and see it's just in a cast. *Thank you, Jesus.*

My left arm feels just as heavy, but when I look, it's not another cast weighing it down. It's a person—more accurately, it's Ethan.

He's asleep on my arm, and when I move it, he shoots up from his seat like someone just screamed in his ear.

"Ethan," I say to get his attention, and his eyes snap to mine. They widen like he can't believe it's me.

"Ave," he says softly, relief evident in his voice. He reaches for me and hugs me as tight as he can without hurting me. "Baby." His voice breaks, and my eyes well with tears.

"Hi," I say, not even sure what's going on right now. I have no idea what day it is, and I couldn't answer most of the questions the doctor would ask if he came in and did that.

"I'm so sorry." Ethan pulls away to look at me. His face shows the grief he feels, my heart clenches, and I want to take away his pain.

"It's okay, Ethan. This wasn't your fault. He thought I was your girlfriend." My cheeks redden, realizing in that moment that we're not still together, and my heart cracks a little more.

"You are my girlfriend." His eyes bore into mine, determination set there.

"Ethan, what happened?" I decide to not argue, mostly because my head can't take it. "Wait, my head hurts—can I have something?"

Ethan moves over me then pushes a button by my shoulder, and a nurse comes into the room almost immediately.

"Oh good! You're awake. We wondered when you'd wake up." She looks nice enough, old enough to be my mom. Dark skin makes her features pop, and she is beautiful with her long hair braided down her back.

She pushes something into the IV in my arm and then hands me a small cup with some pills. I don't even question her, just popping them into my mouth and taking the water from her.

"Your fiancé here was worried sick—I'm so glad you'll be able to talk to him now."

I raise an eyebrow toward Ethan and he looks at me sheepishly. I make a mental note to ask about that later as the nurse finishes checking me out then tells me she's going to send in my doctor.

Staring at my casted arm, I look to Ethan and sigh. "We sure do attract the drama, don't we?" I say it to lighten the mood, and he follows my gaze.

"I can't express to you how truly sorry I am."

Of course, it did the opposite of lighten the mood. "Where is my mom?" I ask suddenly, just realizing she's not here in the room, totally freaking out.

"She's on her way. I texted her when the nurse came in to tell her you're awake. Lucas, Kate, and your grandparents are coming too."

"They all came?"

"Yes. You were kidnapped, Aveline. We didn't know how this was going to go." He looks stricken with grief and even though I have no idea where we truly stand, I don't want him to be hurting.

"I'm sorry, I guess I didn't—"

"You have no reason to be sorry—none." His tone is firm, and he looks angry. "David did this because of me. I put you in this position."

He rests his elbows on his knees and holds his head. I

get why he's taking this so hard; I would feel the same way if it had happened to him.

"It's not your fault," I repeat. "You couldn't have known he was planning this."

He looks at me then and I can tell he wants to tell me something. It's hanging in the air, anxiety written in his features.

"You didn't, right?" Confusion lines my face. I can't put the whole story together, and my head hurts so bad.

"Aveline—" Just then the door flies open and my mother runs over to me. Ethan moves quickly out of her way and she's on me, kissing my head and hugging me the best she can from the odd angle.

"Oh, God, I'm so thankful you're okay." Her relief pours out of her voice, and I peek around to see the rest of my family.

Grandma hugs me next, then Lucas and Kate right after. My grandpa pinches my foot affectionately, his way of saying he's happy I'm okay.

"Just know you're never allowed to do that again—I'm not good at worrying," Lucas says jokingly.

The door opens again and the doctor attempts to enter the room. My family takes up the whole space, and he asks if he can have the room.

Mom stays behind, and I try to catch Ethan's eye, but he leaves before I have the chance. The doctor goes through my vitals and makes sure I'm still functioning like a normal human.

"You are extremely lucky to have such minimal damage to your system," he says.

"I'm still not sure if this is all a dream or not," I say with a slight chuckle in my voice.

"Well, let's get into that a bit." He looks down at the clipboard in his hand and I look to my mom, who gives me a reassuring nod.

"What's your name?"

A smile finds my lips when I think about being in the trunk and thinking about these questions; I never thought I'd actually have to answer them. "Aveline Rose Montgomery."

"And how old are you?"

"Twenty-one."

"What day is it?"

I frown and think. "Uh, Sunday?"

"It's actually Monday—you were sedated for a day to help you heal a little."

"Oh, wow. Guess I missed my flight, huh?" I joke to my mom. She just gives me a timid smile.

"And do you know what happened to you?"

I shift slightly in the hospital bed and think back, blowing out a breath before I recount everything I remember. "Well, we were working an event downtown—wait, where are we?"

"Albuquerque."

My eyebrows shoot up to my hairline. "Wow. He got kind of far, huh?"

The doctor nods and then waits for me to continue my story. "Okay, so, David, who I didn't know was David, came right up to me at the event, I remember that. I recognized him because he found me outside a bar in Acton once." I close my eyes and concentrate. "I went to the bathroom and called Ethan because I thought maybe he knew what was happening, then...well, I left the bathroom, and that's all I remember.

"I woke up and thought I was on a boat because I knew I was moving. Then I figured out I was in a trunk. He stopped once and opened it, and I pretended I was sleeping."

Unexpectedly, tears spring to my eyes, and Mom comes over to hold my hand. I cry for a minute as my brain finally catches up to everything that's happened. Now that I'm safe, it's like I can finally think, and now that I can think, all my emotions are taking a toll.

When I catch my breath, I continue, "I didn't know where we were or how long we'd been driving because I kept passing out. I knew I needed to do something and remembered seeing a show where someone punched out the brake light to get attention." I shrug, not sure what else to say.

"That was smart, and you should be glad you thought of it—it saved your life," my mom tells me.

He gives me a nod. "There are some officers who want to ask some questions—are you feeling up to that?"

I nod, ready to get this over with and go home. "When can I leave?"

"I'd like to keep you here a couple more days to make sure everything's in order. I'd say earliest release would be Wednesday."

The doctor gives us another nod and lets us know we can ask for anything we need. Mom sits next to me and holds my hand as I tilt my head back onto the pillow and let out a sigh.

"I'm so happy you're okay. Ethan and I were worried sick." Mom's eyes glass over but she clears them up a few seconds later.

"When did Ethan get involved?" I'm so behind on the

events of the last few days, and it feels like so much happened when I was unable to participate in real life.

Mom tells me how he basically came to the rescue and gave the police all the help he could, how he drove all the way down here the second they heard about the chase, and how he got hotels and has been taking care of the family the last couple of days.

We catch up on everything, she tells me that the police still can't figure out how he got me out of there without anyone seeing us.

After awhile, I ask her to find me some food; not eating for a day can really make a girl hungry. Before she can leave, though, Ethan and the rest of my crew return to the room, food in hand.

I bide my time with Ethan, eager to talk about what's going to happen with us. We all eat, and everyone seems to be in good spirits. Ethan helps me get situated with my food and stays close in case I need help.

When everyone is finished, they all head to the hotel for the night.

The door closes, and I close my eyes. The few hours I was awake, I talked more than I did the entire week before. My hand twitches when another hand grabs mine, and I open my eyes again. It's no surprise to see Ethan sitting there staring at me, and I know he's ready to talk.

# CHAPTER THIRTY-SEVEN

*Ethan*

ONCE AVELINE'S FAMILY leaves, I take my first real opportunity to come clean about everything I've known the last month about David and his threats.

When I take her hand, she startles and looks at me. She knows I'm about to spill my guts and relaxes into the bed. Her easy demeanor puts me at ease, and I launch into what I need to say.

"I'm sorry about how everything went down," I start. When she opens her mouth, I shake my head, needing to get it out without interruptions, and she nods. "That note you received, those pictures and everything—all of that was David trying to take you from me." Her eyes glass over with confusion but she stays quiet. "After you got the note, I went back over some emails I received and figured out David was behind it all. I confirmed it with a buddy of mine who helped me track him down. Once I found him, I started to follow him, trying to figure out what he was going to do.

"I caught up to him once but he ran, and then I couldn't find him again and he threatened you. I spent the entire night Friday and Saturday morning looking for him and came up completely empty. I decided Saturday I was going to come clean with you. Kate told me where you were, so I was driving to Denver before I even knew what was happening."

She stays silent and processes my words. I hold my breath, hoping this isn't the end. "So, why didn't you answer my call?"

"I couldn't get my fucking phone to charge." I sigh; it's such a lame excuse.

She nods. Her eyes look down at her cast again; it seems to be what draws her attention the most.

"Why did you ignore me?" Her voice breaks when she looks back at me. "Why push me away instead of just explaining what was going on?"

Her eyes brim with tears, the hurt I've inflicted on her coming to the surface. I rub the side of my head. "I don't know...I thought it was the best option to keep you safe."

She just tilts her head back onto her pillow again, blinking her eyes to keep from crying. I think of things I can say and come up with only one thing.

"I love you, Aveline. I know I've screwed up, and I can't even explain how much I want to kick myself for how I handled things. I just hope...I've been praying that you'll forgive me." I grip her hand tighter and stand, leaning over until I meet her eyes.

She meets my gaze, a smile working its way through her tears, and I smile back. "I never stopped loving you, Ethan. I was just really, really pissed at you."

I chuckle and can't wait anymore. Being careful of her cuts and bruises, I press my lips to hers. "I love you so much."

She laughs with me and then winces. "Ouch, I think I need some more pain meds."

I fetch the nurse for her, and once she's comfortable, she drifts off to sleep, her body desperately needing the rest. She's been through hell, and she needs to heal not only physically, but also mentally.

The craziness of the last couple of days—hell, the last few weeks—has taken a toll on all of us. Before I can think things through, my head falls to my chest and I finally rest.

The next few days pass by slowly. The doctors and nurses come and go often, and we don't get much more time alone.

All Aveline's tests come back clean and there's no reason for her to have to stay in the hospital, so we're able to leave. All of us are anxious to get back home and hopefully get back to normal.

David didn't sustain the injuries he should've and was immediately shipped out to some prison in Texas to await his trial. Apparently, he still had a fair shot to plead not guilty, but I'd do anything necessary to make sure he never saw the light of day again.

whisk it all

We're discharged from the hospital and Belle tries to take Aveline, but she refuses to leave my side. I hide my happiness and, with a huff, Belle gets into the other car with her parents and they drive away. Lucas and Kate head back home in her car, and I finally get to spend some time with Aveline alone. Even if it is just us riding in silence, it will at least be peaceful.

"As soon as I get this thing out of a cast, we're going on our trip."

I don't reply, just smile in her direction. She hasn't brought up the trip since we reunited and I'm glad I'm being included, but something in the back of my mind is still bothering me, something her mom mentioned to me.

"What?" she questions when I don't give an answer.

I decide to go for honesty. "You were gonna leave without me?" I try to say it nonchalantly; I don't really have any reason to be mad.

"Well..." she starts, but then she stops, trying to sort through what she's going to say, no doubt. "We were kind of broken up. I didn't want to stay home and wallow in self-pity, and I didn't want to run into you and Marie in town."

She pauses, and I don't answer her, switching lanes to get around a slower car. We process our thoughts in the quiet for a few minutes.

"You actually thought I was with Marie? After everything we've shared?"

She shrugs. "I guess my insecurity got the best of me. I'm sorry, but how about we stay honest with each other from now on, okay? Like the next time someone wants me dead, you actually tell me?" I give her a look and she giggles. "Too soon, huh?"

This whole week with everyone being stuck in the

hospital, we weren't sure how Aveline was going to handle everything and were relieved to learn she hadn't lost her silly sense of humor.

It's funny how something that annoyed me so much at the beginning is something I can't imagine not having in my life now.

I reach over and grab her hand, holding tightly.

We don't get much farther before Aveline is fast asleep. She's been needing a ton of sleep this week, the trauma wearing her down more than she'll ever let on.

My mind wanders to my family, how they would've been there for me like we've been there for her. I think about my mom; Aveline's strength reminds me of her. She never let anything get her down, and I know she would have loved Aveline had she gotten the chance.

I wish more than anything that they could see me, that they could console me in the hard times and be there when I hit milestones, like exiting the military, a big one for me, but then I wouldn't have moved to Colorado. I wouldn't have had to come back here to handle my uncle's place, and I would have missed my chance with Aveline entirely.

So, maybe them passing was necessary. Maybe they see the paths I've taken and know I am on the right one. It feels right, and I think they would be proud of me.

It's several hours and one stop later before we finally get home to Acton. Aveline is now awake and chattering as I pull into her driveway, and she pouts at me. "I thought I'd stay with you tonight."

"Well, we will be staying together. However, I'll be staying with you."

Aveline rolls her eyes. "My family is fine—they're not going to worry about me being at your place."

I bite my lip and chuckle. "Ah, well, that's the thing...I don't actually have a place anymore." The sale was made final last week and the new owners already moved in a couple days ago, but they were very generous and allowed me to hold a few things there due to my circumstances. I didn't think I'd be in a hospital in New Mexico for several days.

"What? It sold already?"

"I was trying to get it sold for money for our trip. Plus, I couldn't exactly travel and keep it going."

"Wow." She stares out the windshield and lets out a breath, looking at her home.

"Let's go, babe."

I get out and run around to help her. Her movements are fine and she's complained more than once about people treating her like a baby, but it still makes me feel better. Stud runs out of the house to greet Aveline, and I see the tears in her eyes, happy to see her dog again.

He looks at me, and I swear that dog puts his claim on her. *Good luck, Stud.*

"You know my family is going to stick you on a couch, just a heads-up." She grins at me then, her eyes sparkling in the moonlight, and I fall just a little harder.

"We'll see about that—I'm pretty chummy with them now." I grin mischievously, and she throws her head back, laughing wildly.

Yup, its official: I love this girl more than anything.

# CHAPTER THIRTY-EIGHT

*Aveline*

IT FEELS SO amazing to be home, to not be in a freaking hospital bed surrounded by people who want to touch you all the time. Why haven't we come up with technology that allows doctors to do their work without touching?
*Touching spreads germs—don't they know that?*
Luckily, though, my injuries weren't as bad as they could have been, so I have to count my blessings and just wait out the next few weeks until I can get this damn cast off.
Ethan and I decided to postpone our trip until January since it would be a pain, not to mention expensive to try to

fly home for the holidays.

I did mention how amazing it would be to spend New Year's Eve in Paris, but when we searched for tickets, my brain about exploded.

I pull onto Main Street, my trusty Jeep trucking along. It's challenging to drive with a broken arm and not exactly something I should be doing, but I had to get out of my house. Its been a couple weeks since we got home and Kate is on her very last day at the bakery, which means today I'm staying wherever she is, regardless of if she wants me there or not.

Her face lights up when I walk in and she runs around the counter to crush me in a hug. I gently remind her that I have some healing ribs that probably shouldn't be crushed. It's something Ethan is taking way too seriously—he won't even consider touching me intimately right now, which is a whole other matter.

"Oh my god! You're here!"

"I know, I had to sneak out."

She gives me a look but smiles. "Well, I'm glad you did! I leave tomorrow." She pouts, and I feel tears stinging my eyes, taking me by surprise.

"I know. I can't believe it. How are you and Lucas doing with it?" At the mention of his name, her eyes dim, and I immediately need to know all the gossip. "What? What is it?"

She sighs and guides me to one of the small tables. There are only a couple of guests in the bakery right now, a slow day.

"Well, we're not doing anything." She rubs a worn spot on the table and looks at me, the expression in her eyes making my heart break for her. "We officially called it off."

"Really? But I thought you guys were going to do the long-distance thing—it's only a couple of hours."

Lucas got into Colorado State University, and he's going for veterinary school. I imagine him not lasting long in that particular major, but I've held back on my thoughts.

"We were, but the more I thought about it, the more I realized I don't want to hold him back. It's a big school, and he'll have so many opportunities. I don't want to tie him to a girlfriend."

I stay silent. I guess I can understand that, but it hurts to see her so sad, and I can't imagine how Lucas is taking it. He's probably really upset; he loves Kate—it's clear as day. After our camping trip, it was undeniable that they had something amazing.

"Well, that's too bad. I hope it can work out."

She shrugs, her eyes on the table, and I decide changing the subject is the only option right now. "So, you'll come home for the holidays, right? We leave in January."

Her eyes light up again and she nods her head. "Of course! I wouldn't miss it this year." We chat a bit more about my trip—sorry, *our* trip—and she tells me all the places I need to visit for her.

When another customer comes in, she goes back up to the counter and helps them. I wander into the back area where all the baking is done, surprised to not see my mom anywhere back here. The kitchen is a mess, and I look around to see how I can help.

I don't even notice how long I'm back there before I see Ethan out of my periphery. I jump slightly and the bowl of water I'm holding spills everywhere. With one arm immobile, I reach for a towel and start cleaning up the mess.

Ethan just leans against a counter and crosses his arms

over his chest, his blue eyes piercing into mine from across the room. He shakes his head and sighs.

"Aveline?"

"Um, yes?" I ask sheepishly.

"What do you think you're doing?" His eyes glare into mine.

"I'm just, ya know, helping out a bit." I finish cleaning up and throw the towel into the overflowing hamper, the one we take home every week to wash.

"You know you're not supposed to be doing this stuff, right?"

I nod my head. "Yeah, but look around." My arm sweeps over the mess in front of me. He takes it in for the first time and his eyebrows furrow.

"Yeah, all right, fine. I'll help you clean this up, but then you're coming home." He points a finger at me, and for a minute I think about what Ethan would be like as a dad. It's a good look on him.

We work together—well, as much as he'll let me help, anyway. The kitchen finally starts to look like a kitchen again and then my mom enters through the back door, again with her arms full. I look at the bags, confused, and Ethan runs over to help her get them onto the counter.

"Mom, why did you buy stuff from the store?"

We normally get our stuff in bulk orders that are delivered right to the bakery so we can save money and not have to haul everything ourselves.

"Oh, well, we must have missed an order sheet. They weren't able to squeeze me in this week, so I'm having to run around until they can deliver next week." She finally looks up at us and frowns at the kitchen. "You cleaned up?"

"Mom," I say, waiting until she looks at me. "You need

extra help."

"Oh, honey, I know. I just haven't had the time to hire anyone."

"What happened to the person who was going to replace me?"

She looks at her bags again and doesn't answer the question. Ethan looks at me, and I can see what his eyes say: she doesn't have anyone lined up.

"Mom, you don't have anyone, do you?"

She sighs and looks at me, defeated. "No, honey, I don't."

I stand there in silence, the confession throwing me off. This whole time I thought she had someone coming in and helping her with the baking and the general running of things, but she is planning to do it all alone.

"Okay, well, I'm coming back to help." I hold up my good arm up to stop the protesting I know I'm about to hear from them both. "I can run a mixer with one hand and you need the help. We have a few months until we leave, and we'll find someone before then. Besides, I'm not working."

"I'll help too." Mom and I both look to Ethan, her with shock and me with a smile. He's a good one. *I think I'll keep him.* He looks at her and says, "You all are letting me stay with you for free and you're feeding me your food, so please, let me come in and help. I can come with Aveline some mornings and give you a break."

She looks like she's about to cry, but being the woman she is, she blinks them back and nods at us. "That would be amazing, thank you."

With that decided, we finish helping her in the kitchen then head home to get ready for the night. The family is throwing Kate a going-away dinner, and we have to get ready for it.

Hand in hand, Ethan and I head out to his truck. Before he can hoist me into the cab, I grab his face with my good hand and kiss the daylights out of him.

*I'm definitely keeping this one.*

---

The night is wonderful. We make Kate a gourmet meal, we talk the entire evening, we laugh, and inevitably, I cry.

Lucas and Kate don't speak to each other the entire time, and as much as I want to interfere, I can't fix their problems. Lucas watches her the whole night, though, and my heart aches for the love he feels like he's losing.

Going their separate ways is hard for them both, and as much as I understand Kate's point, I don't agree with it.

When she gets ready to leave, Lucas disappears without a goodbye, and Kate's eyes well with tears when she looks at me. She shakes her head and shrugs.

"I'm going to miss you so much," I say. Grabbing her shoulders with one arm, I squeeze her tight. She rubs my back, and I hear her sniff into my hair. We stand there for a few minutes, just crying on each other, not quite ready to let go.

"I'll be back as soon as I can, and plus, your trip will make this first year fly," she tells me as she pulls back. The rest of the family takes their turns saying goodbye, even Ethan. She steps back and punches his arm then points a finger in his face. "You take care of our girl."

He chuckles. "I will, don't worry."

Then, she runs down the steps and gets into her car. A few tears escape my eyes as I watch her drive down the driveway. I look up to Lucas' window and see him standing there, watching her leave.

I send up a quick prayer that some day, they'll find their happiness, no matter where it comes from.

# CHAPTER THIRTY-NINE

*Aveline*
8 weeks later

"AH, THIS FEELS so freaking good." I'm unable to contain the moan that escapes my lips at the most wonderful feeling in the universe. "This is better than anything I've ever felt!" I exclaim, looking over at Ethan.

He chuckles at me. "Really? Anything?"

I blush and look at my newly released and fully healed arm. "Well, almost." Being able to feel and look at my arm felt miraculous; finally being able to scratch my arm…well, that is *pure heaven*.

We're driving home to my grandparents' house. I had thought living there with Ethan would be weird, but so far, everyone has acted normal enough.

They moved him into Lucas' room when he left for college, but Ethan manages to sneak across the hall most nights. *Okay, every night.*

Everyone is getting along great. He cooks and cleans whenever it's needed, and he helps my grandpa on the farm every day. I am starting to think they will miss him more than they'll miss me when we leave for Europe.

We finally found someone to help my mom out at the bakery, and that was a godsend because doing it one-handed was no easy feat.

With my arm newly liberated from its prison, I will be able to help her out now that all the crazy holidays are quickly approaching.

It's the first week of November, and Thanksgiving is coming up fast. Our family plans for it the entire month.

Instead of the traditional family Thanksgiving most have, we do one for the entire town. It started about twenty years ago and was something my dad thought up. Everyone who couldn't afford their own Thanksgiving could come to the town event. It started small but is now the largest holiday for Acton.

It's called the Jackson Montgomery Thanksgiving, and it's tradition to honor him. Almost every family comes to it now. We hold it in the old mill, where we had Ethan's party, because it is the largest place in Acton and we never fully know the number of people who will show up.

Last year, we hosted over three hundred people. The prediction is something like four hundred this year, though.

I smile as I think about my dad and how happy he would be that the whole town chips in and not a single soul goes without for the holiday.

We pull up the driveway and jump out of the truck. The

house is seemingly always full for the month of November, and every person on the planning committee comes here for instructions on what they are supposed to contribute.

"Okay, Meryl, you'll get the decorations for the tables, and Sally, can you handle getting a headcount? I know it's a big job, but we need to make sure we have enough food." Mom oversees organizing everyone; she's carried it on since Dad passed, and I know she does it to make him proud.

I try to sneak past the living room full of ladies sipping hot chocolate and eating freshly baked cookies so I can just go upstairs, but as I step onto the first step, Ethan's hand firmly grasped in mine, my name is called out.

Hiding my cringe, I paste a smile on and turn to them. Most of them get up and hug me, congratulating me on my arm that's finally free. The others, however, fawn over my boyfriend like I'm not even there.

When the proper greetings have all been exchanged, we head up the stairs.

"I think I got volunteered for about fifty jobs just now," Ethan grumbles behind me. There's no doubt about one thing: Ethan is officially the town's favorite hero.

Thanksgiving has arrived, and the mill is completely packed. Almost every single family, couple, and single is squished in here for the meal, and I smile broadly at the next family in line to get their turkey.

We ended up needing a lot of food—like *a lot*. I believe there was something like fifty turkeys, and I'm not even sure where we found that many, but everyone pitched in with buying and cooking them. The sides are also in abundance, and there's an entire wall of tables filled with platters and drink dispensers. It's a madhouse, and I've never seen my mom so freaking happy.

"Hey there, hot stuff." I feel hands on my hips and turn slightly to see a flushed Ethan.

"Oh my gosh, where have you been?" I ask, placing more slices of turkey on someone's plate as they move through the line.

"Oh, well, Mrs. Mason needed help with the drinks… then the tables…then the chairs…and then the decorations," he says, giving me a look.

I quirk an eye at him. "None of those were her jobs." I laugh at his expense; it's probably not nice, but the fact that Mrs. Mason is using him as her call boy cracks me up.

"That's just great." He rests his forehead on the back of my neck, and it feels right.

When the line finally starts dwindling after about two hours of serving, we take whatever is left and find our own seat. Lucas is here as well, having come up the mountain from school for the week. I am so excited to see him, and I hadn't realized the comedic relief we were missing, but having him back makes everything feel perfect.

Mom finds herself a seat by us, and Grandma and Grandpa have already finished their meal. It's probably my favorite Thanksgiving since Dad died, and I know a lot of that has to do with the guy sitting beside me.

"No Kate this year?" I ask Lucas, assuming they've been in contact.

"How would I know?" he grumbles. I haven't talked to him about Kate since he got home, but I didn't think it was a sore subject.

"Um, darn. I guess she couldn't make it," I say to Ethan. He saw how Lucas responded and nods his head at me. I shrug and drop the subject. Not long after, Lucas gets up and stomps out of the mill, and I look after him sadly.

"It'll be okay, babe." Ethan wraps his arm around my shoulder, seeing how sad I am to see Lucas upset.

After we've finished, people begin to come over to our table, profusely thanking my mom for the lovely dinner and sharing memories of my dad. I see her eyes glistening more than once and know she's proud of the work she's done.

We stand and make our way toward the exit so we can say goodbye to everyone who came out, wishing them happy holidays and safe travels.

When the last of the groups leave, we turn toward the mess that is left behind. Many of the town folk are helping with giant trash bags and takeout containers for the leftovers.

I look at Ethan and see him rubbing his knee. "You don't have to stay and help, hon—you've done enough."

He shoots me a wink and holds open his own trash bag. Together we work on cleaning everything up. With all the help, it doesn't take much time at all, and soon we're on our way home, all of us exhausted.

Lying down on my bed, I let out a long content sigh and breath easily, knowing what a successful holiday we had and hoping Ethan is okay after being on his leg all day, running around from place to place.

A smile hits my lips when I hear my door creak open and feel him slide in next to me. He wraps one arm under my head and the other over my stomach, our usual cuddle position.

With that feeling of happiness overwhelming me, I fall into a deep sleep, feeling grateful for my perfect life.

# EPILOGUE

*Ethan*

THE SNOW FALLS heavily all around. Standing there with a mug of coffee warming my bones, the house quiet early on this Christmas morning, I think about my parents, wondering as I always do if they would be proud of the things I've done, and most importantly, of the thing I will be doing in the future. I'm not sure exactly how life will play out, don't know if things are going to go as planned. As I think of the past, I know it's not very likely.

I take a sip and smile at the present I got for Aveline—well, I should say, *presents*. I'm pretty sure she'll be blown away, and I can't wait to see her face when she opens them.

Heading back into the kitchen, I pull out the ingredients for what the family planned for breakfast and start heating up the griddle to make some pancakes. Stud takes a seat right at me feet, ready for any scraps that might fall.

I chuckle to myself at the scenario. Making Aveline's family breakfast on Christmas morning—I never would have thought I would be here. Nevertheless, I feel like this is where I'm supposed to be, and I'll forever be grateful for that.

This family is mine now. I don't have to go through Aveline or wait for an invitation to anything; they always welcome me, no matter what.

Just as I'm pouring the first pancake, Belle comes in, her robe wrapped tightly around her.

"Merry Christmas, Ethan," she says lovingly as she pours a cup of coffee for herself. Surveying where I'm at with breakfast, she jumps in and starts the bacon. Not long after, Grandma and Grandpa, who have asked me to start calling them that, shuffle in as well.

Grandpa goes to the table while Grandma pours him some coffee and starts the eggs. With everything under control with breakfast, I start to let my mind wander to a little later when I'll be giving Aveline her presents.

Just as the last pancake comes off the griddle, Lucas and Aveline both come into the kitchen, rubbing their eyes. Aveline walks up to me, and I shamelessly kiss her on the lips.

I think she forgets her family is watching because she responds to me easily, and when she pulls away, her cheeks heat with embarrassment as Lucas groans his disgust.

"Merry Christmas, baby," I tell her, giving her hip a squeeze.

"Merry Christmas," she murmurs, a grin plastered to

her face.

We sit at the table and pass around plates to get them all filled up, and everyone starts chatting about this, that, and the other. As I sit and listen to the conversation, a thought hits me.

*This is my life and I freaking love it.*

When breakfast is over, we clear the table and head into the family room to gather around the tree. Once we're all situated, Belle starts handing out gifts, and I'm shocked when she hands one to me.

Whispering a thank you, I tear open the package. Emotions clog my throat and I try to swallow them down as best I can.

Staring at me are my parents, or a picture of them, rather. It's an old photo of us. I was just in grade school, and we look like the perfect all-American family. The image has been blown up and printed on a canvas.

I clear my throat and look at Belle; her eyes are teary as she waits for my response. "This is perfect. Thank you so much."

She nods and waves me off like it's no big deal.

Aveline thinks all the presents have been handed out, but I have one more to give. Reaching behind the tree, I retrieve the envelope I hid there.

I hand it to her and wait.

She eyes me curiously. "What's this?"

I smile at her. "Open it," I say. "I think you'll be surprised." She puts a finger under the flap and pulls out the contents. She frowns at first then looks at me. "Look closer," I tell her. When she does, she sees it.

"Tomorrow?" Aveline looks at me like she's about to explode.

"Yup. It took some doing, but I got them." I smile at her, proud of my gift. Jumping out of her seat, she nearly knocks me over, but I correct my stance in time and wrap my arms around her.

"Ethan, this is perfect!" She looks at them and then at her family. "We leave for Paris tomorrow!"

She looks at me again with an expression I've seen a hundred times, one I'll never grow tired of seeing.

One day, I'll make it a permanent fixture in my life. Someday soon I'll make Aveline my wife, but until then, I'll cherish the love she's giving me now, the home she's provided by accepting me as part of the family.

She walks over, standing right in front of me. "I love you, Ethan Hart."

I grin, unable to help myself. "And I love you, Aveline Montgomery."

Maybe she'll be my wife sooner than I think, but for now, here's to Paris.

The End

## ACKNOWLEDGEMENTS

First and foremost, thank you to everyone who took the time to read this book. It's been a long time coming for me and I can't wait to dip my toes in many more to come.

To the person who made this possible; my husband. I know it's not easy to watch the toddler every night after work so that I can have my dream, it doesn't go unnoticed, you are seriously the best.

To my family, those who know about this anyway, (I'm looking at you, mom) thank you for the support and encouragement. Writing a book is daunting, and having anyone read it is scary as hell, but I was never doubted.

-J.S.

To get all the exclusives on giveaways, book signings, and new releases, sign up for the newsletter! Only sent a few times a year.

Join her reader group for all the shenanigans: https://www.facebook.com/groups/2126853240907148/

Or stalk her on her many social media platforms:
BookBub
Goodreads
Facebook
Instagram
Twitter

Other titles by J.S. Wood
The Anti-Love Agents
Take My Hand
Got Your Six

Pre-Order Now
Follow My Lead


Shift: A Driven Novel
Kickstart: A Driven Novel (Coming June 2021)

The Montgomery Family

Whisk It All
One More Shot

## ABOUT THE AUTHOR

J.S. Wood has been writing contemporary romance for four years and enjoys giving you the happily ever after we all deserve, while at the same time delivering you humor and occasionally, some suspense. Her love of romance novels inspired her to write her own. When she's not writing, she's playing with the family, hiking in the Rocky Mountains, or dreaming with her husband, two young kids and an abundance of animals. Their dream is to one day get their own fully sustainable farm.

"Nothing happens unless first a dream." – Carl Sandburg

Keep up with her at www.jswoodauthor.com

Made in the USA
Columbia, SC
24 May 2022